I0725668

RELIEF

a novel

Klaus Jakelski

Relief
Copyright © 2019 Klaus Jakelski
All rights reserved
Published by Blue Denim Press Inc.
First Edition
ISBN 978-1-927882-46-7
No part of this book may be used or reproduced in any manner whatsoever without written permission except in the case of brief quotations embodied in critical articles or reviews.

This is a work of fiction. Any resemblance to events, organizations, or to people living or dead, is entirely coincidental and beyond the intent of the author or the publisher.

Cover Design: Robert Scozzari/Typeset in Windlass, Cambria and Garamond

Library and Archives Canada Cataloguing in Publication
Title: Relief : a novel / Klaus Jakelski.
Names: Jakelski, Klaus, 1951- author.
Identifiers: Canadiana (print) 20190150955 | Canadiana (ebook) 20190150971 | ISBN 9781927882467
   (softcover) | ISBN 9781927882474 (Kindle) | ISBN 9781927882481 (EPUB)
Classification: LCC PS8619.A3695 R45 2019 | DDC C813/.6—dc23

In memory of

Lt. Colonel Nelson L. A. Wagner
"A soldier's soldier"

In *Relief*, Klaus Jakelski delivers another taut, richly-imagined thriller. The prose is elegant and the tension cranks steadily toward an intense—and surprising—climax.
    —**Sean Costello**, author of *Here After*

ONE

Frank couldn't concentrate. Endlessly shifting in his seat. Unable to sleep. The droning of the engines prodding him toward slumber, and momentarily pulling him back.

The flight from Ramstein was under two hours, but the accommodations of a military transport were not meant for comfort. The Hercules had only a few other passengers, and he hadn't struck up a conversation with a single one. Perhaps he hadn't cared to. Or, it simply wasn't in him.

He had been uncomfortable for some time, not just on this flight. He might even admit that he was anxious about his new deployment. But he wouldn't tell anybody about the feeling in his gut. The churning that had gone on for weeks. The need for antacids. Asking one of his colleagues for some major medication, before he left home.

None of that. He'd never let on.

Most of the horror he had witnessed on his last mission had been washed from his soul, either by drink or some other alchemy he didn't understand. The shifting sands of time burying painful memories, as they always did, until the ripples were unexpectedly revealed again, by a sudden rain.

He looked around the inside of the plane. The mass of cargo that was strapped down in the cavernous back, the few rows of seats along the side of the forward fuselage, with the wide aisle up the middle. Only a few of the seats ahead occupied by heads of hair. Some shaved, some long. Heads perched on torsos clad in military fatigues. None of whom he wanted to get to know.

The cockpit door was open, so he could see the pilots sitting up high on the flight deck, their animated conversation visible but inaudible.

The droning of the engines resonating in his ears. As if they wanted to take him to another place, far away from here. Causing him to turn his head. Struggling to stay awake, or to try and sleep. He didn't know which. Until that vague scent twigged him. Was it unwashed khakis or sun burnt uniform? He didn't know and it didn't matter. Suddenly, it was as if he wasn't even on the plane. Unaware of anything around him, he was locked inside his consciousness. A prisoner in a place he could never quite remember. One that never let him go.

The smell.

That smell!

There was no escaping the smell along the red dirt road. The savannah grass, yellowed since spring, rustled whenever it brushed his fatigues. The odd tree, green against the burnt African countryside, rose from the steep river bank.

Frank Lambert looked at the river. Bloated black bodies bobbed along in the gentle current of brown water. The banks were littered with bodies as far as he could see.

Too late again.

Why bother looking?

The occasional black man armed with a gun or a machete walked the dusty road, oblivious to the carnage. Uncaring passage between the body parts—the spilled blood—the disembowelled bellies. And the smell. The smell of flesh and blood, bowels and urine rotting in the hundred-and-ten-degree sun.

But the warriors, oblivious, walked like ghosts.

A momentary gust of wind felt like the devil's own breath on his back.

Then it happened. A voice? He strained to hear above the rustling of the grass and the noise of the crickets. Was he fooling himself? Again, he strained. Did he hear, "*Aider moi.*"?

A few yards farther along the river, he stopped to listen.

"'Elp me," came softly from the river's edge.

Frank hurried down the dusty grass, sending snakes slithering and rats scurrying out of the way, and stood on the soft bank.

"*Aider moi!*" He heard the stifled urgency.

He turned over the body on his left. Dead. He pivoted to the one on the right and turned it over.

The naked man held up his left arm. "'Elp me!" The right arm limp with bullet wounds.

Rustling grass startled Frank. He turned to see a black man running at him with a machete. A tight fist caught him hard in the centre of the red cross on his T-shirt, thrusting him into the river.

Frank coughed as he slipped on the mud, struggling back up the bank.

"'Elp me!" came the panicked voice. The injured black man looked straight at Frank.

The warrior in the loincloth held his hand up to Frank and raised his long blade. He let it drop and severed the injured man's left arm.

The cry silenced the crickets.

The cry dissected Frank's soul.

He covered his ears but it did no good. He was living in the scream.

The warrior seemed to delight in Frank's anguish. Watching him. Laughing. Waving the machete over his head. Then he turned and slashed an X deep into the screaming man's abdomen. He waited a long moment. With one more thrust he severed head and body. Blood sprayed up the embankment. Blood ran everywhere!

Frank took his hands from his ears.

Finally, in silence, the sound of the crickets returned.

Furiously, the warrior grabbed Frank's shoulder and shook him as he raised his machete. His eyes became two black holes into an empty skull. The crazed man was inches from his face, shouting, hyperventilating. Spraying his face with spit. His mouth a jagged hole with two reptilian eyes inside. A python lashed out at him, missing its mark as he pulled back.

But the warrior's voice was becoming more and more distant, until Frank couldn't hear him any more. All he felt were hammering fists thrusting into his chest and shoulder. Pushing him back farther. Deeper into the river. Closer and closer to the bodies floating by. He looked back. The water was ready to swallow him up, like it had a will of its own, wanting him to join the dead.

Come. Come, it said.

When he heard the distant sound of aircraft engines, his heart sped up even more and pounded from his chest up into his neck. It filled his throat.

Panicking, Frank felt caught. Stuck somewhere in a place he dreaded.

The decrescendo of turbo-props and the sound of rushing air surrounded him.

What's happening?

His hands clawed at something behind him.

The black man shook him by the shoulder.

Frank pulled himself back in panicked retreat against the outer wall of the transport plane, soaked with perspiration.

Electric motors whirred in the fuselage. The plane pitched. The sound of rushing air quickened.

"Are you all right, sir?" The black officer in khaki fatigues cocked his head to the side as he wiped Frank's face with a tissue. "You sure you're okay?" He looked Frank over for a moment as if he needed to be certain. He said, "Sorry to rush you, sir. Got to buckle up. We're landing in Sarajevo."

He took a few deep breaths. Frank Lambert composed himself as he peered out the window over the bright blue Mediterranean. His heart slowed as rapidly as the plane lost altitude. Momentarily, the twinkling highlights of the Mediterranean shoreline disappeared, along with his memory.

TWO

The giant fan blades spoke to him quietly as they slowly went around, *Whup—Whup—Whup.*

He could hear them clearly as if he had tuned out all the other sounds in the room. He followed the tip of one fan blade, that was right above him, around and slowly around in its hypnotic path.

They only spoke to him. *Whup—Whup—Whup.* As if they were ignoring everybody else in the room.

Frank, a tall athletic man with an angular face framed by a shock of dark hair, was lying there, stretched out on the wooden bench with his head propped up on his duffel bag. His hands folded on his abdomen. A habit from too many years of scrubbing and gowning and waiting for the patient to be ready. The surgeon's hands not allowed near his neck, or below his waist, in order to maintain sterility.

This building however, was not sterile. Frank's habit was just that——a surgeon's affectation. He was entirely unaware of the position of his hands.

Looking up, he had counted them. Twenty-four fans. All rotating at the same speed in the same direction, about eighty feet above his head.

All saying, *Whup—Whup—Whup,* to him alone.

As he dropped his guard, the general din of the room intruded into his private space. Slowly, increasing its volume until it drowned out the ceiling fans. The disjointed sound of many crowded people coming together in a cacophony.

The new groups had been assembled in this hangar at Sarajevo Airport, purportedly to wait for their rides out to their final destinations. The night before, they had slept on cots in another hangar. About a hundred and fifty of them, sharing the space, the cold food, the nooks and crannies of the building, as well as stale cigarette smoke, and the few bathrooms.

The UN had opted to keep them here because Sarajevo was being held hostage by snipers. Even the west end of the runway wasn't safe from their bullets. One of *them* had put a fifty caliber round through their plane's tail fin. A repeat occurrence.

But today the roads to the north were to be cleared of the Bosnian Serb forces that held the city for ransom, and the waiting groups were supposed to get out.

Frank could hardly wait to get to his mission, a tiny abandoned village south-west of Banja Luka. But what he really wanted, what his body and soul were now craving, was the simple relief a shower would bring.

They had been called together by UN officials seated to one side of the colossal hanger at a simple wooden table. One officer spoke into a microphone, and the words echoed around the building that was large enough to hold a jumbo jet.

When he said, "Forward Doctors International. Group number three," Frank followed the echoes around the building. His eyes drifted over drums of lubricant, tool lockers, boarding and repair ramps arranged around the walls. Rows of frosted windows were evenly divided below the ceiling. Their colour betrayed an overcast day.

From around the room, twenty-two people including Frank, straggled over to the announcement desk. They were each given a yellow armband and asked to wait.

So much for the morning's excitement.

Their group also had five men in uniform, with sidearms. Some wearing the signature pale blue helmet of the UN.

One, with a colonel's insignia and a patch that read, *Richter,* went from the desk directly back to his bench and lay back on his duffel bag, with his arms behind his head and his cap pulled over his face. He hadn't spoken to anybody. The blue helmet hung opposite from his makeshift pillow. A holstered nine millimeter hung loosely from his belt.

Frank had heard about Colonel Richter before, but he had never met him. And it looked like he wasn't going to speak to him now. Maybe later.

Richter's reputation preceded him. Tough, even for a protector of an NGO. In this case, UNPROFOR, the United Nations Protective Force in Yugoslavia, protecting Frank's group. A hard German who apparently played by the book.

For a moment, he wondered whether Richter heard the fans too?

The surgeon was feeling pride in serving with the colonel. Even though, as he looked at Richter reclined on his bench, with his cap over his face and his pistol hanging from his belt, Frank wished he had his own sidearm.

Frank sat back down on his bench and looked over at the yellow group. They had all come together a short distance away and were making some introductions. He thought about joining them, but dismissed the idea and decided instead to watch for a while.

One man, wearing khakis without insignia, was clearly different from the rest. He had a cherubic face and sparse hair. His hands were very animated and his speech was rapid as he smiled. His feet continuously moved as he spoke and engaged every member of the group.

Must be a priest.

Because Frank was from Boston, his mind added, *Movements, gestures and words that could hide a thousand wrongs. Like he's been branded.*

Letting his eyes drift, he noticed her. Tall and slender, her khakis setting off her black skin; she was not overly engaged with her group. She also wore a yellow armband.

Frank watched intently. She carried herself well, walking through the group.

The moment came when she saw him staring. She locked Frank's eyes, and for a scant instant, her face softened. Then, as if she had betrayed herself, she abruptly turned away.

Frank lay back down and closed his eyes. The fans were ignoring him now.

The din of the room and the overhead announcements danced around him, playing with him, distracting him.

Frank might have preferred the secret message from the ceiling; instead he wondered about the woman for a while, and decided that he somehow knew her. Or did he?

THREE

"Incoming wounded, sir." The duty sergeant lingered long enough in the doorway to be sure the surgeon was awake, then gently closed the door.

Frank Lambert sat up in bed, fully dressed. He ran some water in the corner sink, rinsed his face, and smoothed back his dark hair.

There had been no wounded in the weeks since he had arrived. Frank wondered…

Crossing the dark square, he could hear the distant howl and whine of a diesel truck working its gears against the mountains. At least the ground was dry.

Frank let himself into the heavy wooden door and said, "What kind of trouble tonight?"

"One wounded. French infantry from the 16th district. Injured leg." The duty sergeant turned to his papers. "Field-triaged as surgical."

"French infantry?" said Frank, disappointed. *French foot soldier.* He leaned on the radio table with both hands and studied a deep crack in the wall.

"The road to Sarajevo is heavily mined——we're the closest site."

The grating whine of the truck was getting closer.

"Get Sergeant Pakin in here. Let the others sleep. I'll assess this."

"Yes, sir." The duty sergeant got up to go. "Mind the radio, sir?"

"No problem."

Frank went into the operating room, changed, and checked the drugs and supplies. *Minimal but adequate.*

The nurse soon appeared. "Doctor." She paused, looking at him from the back. "What's up?"

"Evening." He turned to her. "We'll know shortly if it's a good evening or not." He gave her the details.

"You think it's getting worse?" she said, getting behind the screen curtain in the corner of the room to change. She obviously knew his views.

Frank didn't answer. He looked over the order lists but caught the odd glimpse of bare black skin through the inadequate cover.

Gwen Pakin emerged in her greens just as they heard the squeal of the truck's brakes outside.

In the dark, two soldiers wearing blue UN helmets were barely discernible through the swirling dust. They were clearing away the tarpaulin at the back of the truck.

Frank strode over to them. "I'm Frank Lambert, surgeon in charge."

"Sir!" the younger man answered with a perfect Oxford accent. "Our orders." He handed over a packet.

"Bring him in the side door." He motioned. "Hurry. Snipers."

Frank guided them to the side of the two-storey building, past the canvas-curtained windows leaking yellow light at the edges. Once inside, he studied the papers as the patient was prepared.

Transfer in order. Serial number 463-579-549. Male. Serving sixteenth precinct UNPROFOR, French battalion. Twenty-two years old. Eighty-four kilograms. Born in Orange. *There's a nice place.* Roman Catholic. No allergies. Injury—Right leg below knee—Land mine—1740 hours. Serology negative. No blood or blood products given. Jacques Ribout.

"Hey!" Frank shouted at the medics before they left. "You guys give him anything?"

"Fifteen of morphia at 2247 hours," Oxford said from the far side of the truck, "and the IV of Ringers Lactate at 150 CCs per hour."

"No blood or substitutes?"

"Nothing. Sir…"

"Yeah, I know. Supplies are low. Road is mined." He hung his head.

"Sir, I'm sorry."

Frank caught himself. "Don't be, soldier. I'm having a bad night. Not you."

Shortly, the nurse had the patient ready and they were gowned at his side. The makeshift operating room was kept permanently ready. To get it going required only pulling down disposable blue plastic sheets over the walls and getting the instruments out. Passable as a battlefield operating room, not as a secondary location. But…

The surgeon inspected the draped wound. "I'm going to give you something to get you in the mood, soldier." He injected some Versed into the IV.

"*Docteur, ma jambe?*"

"*Ta jambe est fini.*" He hoped his French was good enough. He added, "Wasted."

Jacques Ribout began to cry uncontrollably, and Pakin consoled him, leaning down and cradling his head. "Think we should get someone else in here?" she said.

"Give him a minute." They did, and Lambert held up a syringe. "Ketamine. Great battlefield drug. Has been for decades." He gave the full syringe intravenously, and the patient became docile and tranquil, although he remained awake.

"The problem," Lambert explained, "is that although the leg is only missing up to mid-calf, the bone is splintered all the way up to the knee and most likely into the knee. All that's going to happen if I amputate below the knee is that infection is going to set in, and you know our situation with antibiotics."

She nodded at him and turned her attention back to Ribout.

"So, we'll take it here," Lambert started to cut with his scalpel just below an inflatable tourniquet, round the entire thigh. He cut through the muscle and tissues, tying off blood vessels as he went.

"*Tout va bien,* Jacques?" (Everything okay, Jacques?)

The soldier, off in his own world, replied, "*Oui.*"

Frank worked quickly and carefully. After sawing through the bone, he sewed together the remaining flaps of tissue and applied a tight bandage.

"That will do," he said. "We'll carry him through the night with fifteen of morphine every two to eight hours. Cut the IV to 125 CCs an hour." He turned to the door and shouted, "Sergeant."

The duty sergeant helped move Ribout back onto the gurney and onto the bed in the small adjoining recovery room.

Frank and Gwen Pakin looked to the last details before giving him the first fifteen of morphine and raising the side rails of the hospital bed. It was 0315 hours.

"Okay, Sergeant. He's in your hands. If you need me, you know where I am."

"Right." She turned toward a cot in the corner and momentarily glanced back at him, as if she were wondering what he was thinking. "Goodnight, Frank."

"'Night, Gwen." He left without looking at her.

"I need to meet with Colonel Richter in the morning," he said to the duty sergeant on the way out. "Any time he's free. Wake me."

"I'll do what I can, sir."

"Goodnight."

Frank stopped halfway across the square and looked around at the rolling contours of the mountaintops, nicely outlined by the threatening light of the moon. The romantic glow that could give him up to a sniper. He glanced back at the main building and noticed that the light leaking around the recovery room window suddenly darkened. He quickly walked to his building, slapped the dust off his clothes and went inside before the moon could betray him.

His room was dark. The window facing the square had shutters instead of a tarpaulin, and he opened them so he could just see out.

Exhausted, he lay down on his bed, putting his hands behind his head.

Unable to sleep, Frank thought about Gwen. He thought about her upturned eyes, her angular jaw, and the shallow dimples that framed her full lips. The shock of short straight hair that gave her an almost exotic look. He'd rather she wasn't bunking with the patient. But it was other things that interested him more. Particularly, what she had told him some nights ago.

After ten days at the new deployment, Frank's curiosity had prevailed. It was more like he had gotten hooked.

They had sat down to talk at his table, after leaving the canteen.

Gwen told him she too had been on the Rwanda mission. Only thing, back then her hair had been half an inch long and tight with curls.

That explained why he didn't recognise her at the airport.

She also alluded to his wild behaviour after work, on that deployment.

Which explained her turning away from him at the airport.

Frank had told her he'd had a rough time, but was better now.

Apparently she could see that.

Then she told him about her mission to Chechnya, to help the Russians, and a man she had met there. Like she wanted everything out on the table.

Frank had responded by telling her he was separated now.

Before she left for her quarters Gwen had looked at him, pulled him close and kissed him lightly on the cheek.

He had to wonder about her in the operating room though, changing into greens. Did she want him to see as much as he did?

Frank didn't want to lay there like this until dawn, again, speculating...

Might as well get up.

He sat on a counter by the window, looked over at the recovery room window, and pulled a hidden pack of cigarettes off the wall shelf. Matches were stuffed in the cellophane. He lit one, pulled his legs up and inhaled deeply. He held up the cigarette and watched the red ember glow.

FOUR

A mixed morning. Sun and cloud—not warm, not cold—feeling damp like it might rain, but the dust a testament to the dry spell. A typical Balkan fall morning. Frank threw open his shutters the rest of the way and took a deep breath. At least he had managed to sleep past nine.

He wandered out in his crumpled greens, down the square to the food hut. He asked Dayna to make him some bread with cheese and an extra black coffee. He ducked a low beam and sat with Gwen, who was on her third cup, at a small wooden table.

"Ribout did well," she said, looking tired. "Pressure was good all night and his pain control adequate. No unusual bleeding, just a bit of ooze. Temp's fine. O2 sats over 95."

Even though she looked tired, her upturned eyes and high cheek bones were framed to advantage by her falling locks.

Frank said, "Thanks. I'll see him later."

"You're still pissed!" She waited for an answer. "Aren't you?" She pursed her narrow mouth.

He looked away to deflect her comment and caught the big black cook, scowling at her assistant, Jennifer. But the sous-chef didn't seem to be doing anything wrong.

Jennifer was about a foot shorter than Dayna, well muscled with blonde hair cut a quarter of an inch long, as if she were a commando.

She brought the coffee to the table. When Frank saw her looking at him, she averted her gaze and hurried away. The coffee was strong. The bread followed shortly, covered with some kind of local blue cheese, partly melted, the way he liked it. He ate in silence.

Gwen watched intently. Perhaps his lips were quivering more than usual.

"Situation's not good, Gwen!"

She shrugged. "I just follow orders. Keeps me sane."

Frank wanted to say, *You're Army*, but thought better of it. He concentrated on his food and ate in silence.

The duty sergeant came in after a while and said, "Colonel Richter will see you any time you're ready."

"Be there shortly."

"Yes, sir." He turned and left.

Frank cupped his hands around his coffee and swirled it for a moment, watching the oily droplets of caffeine dancing on the dark surface. Finally, he said to Gwen, "No time like the present," and walked to the door.

Frank looked back and saw that she was watching him go. She always seemed to be watching him go—Frank knew that. This time she looked like she wanted to say something, perhaps to make him feel better, but... maybe concerned about how he would reply... possibly wondering about the source of his anger.

Richter's office was above the duty sergeant's and the operating room. The building, in typical Bosnian country style, was an A-frame above the main floor, so his office had two sloping timber walls of great height and two flat walls with shuttered and blanketed windows. As a result, it was lit in the tungsten colour of light bulbs and the orange glow off the tarpaulins covering the windows.

"Come in." Frank opened the heavy wooden door, and Richter gestured. "Sit down."

"Thank you, Kurt." He sat on a green leather armchair in front of the great clean desk.

"So, how is the patient? I understand everything went well." He spoke with a heavy Austrian accent, not unlike Schwarzenegger.

"Oh yeah. No problem."

"Then…" Richter gestured with an upturned hand.

"Well…" Frank looked at the poker face for a moment. Blue eyes under short crew cut blonde hair with large lips. "The question isn't whether this patient is doing well."

"Rather?"

"The question is why we're doing *this* patient at all?"

"We do what we can to help." Richter, a rather tall man, sat sprawled on a creaky rocker behind his light coloured oak desk.

"I'm talking about our mandate." Frank tapped his palm. "We're supposed to be assisting civilian casualties of war."

"Not this again. What civilian casualties of war?"

"That," said Frank, "is exactly my point. Forward Doctors International were deployed here under the United Nations Protective Force, far in advance of the rest, to assist with civilian casualties where they occur. We haven't seen a single one! We're getting injured soldiers instead—injured UN soldiers."

"Exactly. And we must do the humanitarian thing for them, mustn't we? Besides, supplies are—"

"Yeah I know. Supplies are low. Lines are down. Road is mined. Bullshit this. Bullshit that. Bullshit-bullshit, bullshit-bullshit!"

Richter bolted upright to the loud protest of his chair. "Frank, it's a good thing you're not a soldier!"

Richter's look penetrated him. Frank felt a pearl of perspiration run down his back.

Colonel Richter drew in a deep, calming breath, as if he was thinking about his only surgeon; and rethinking. He exhaled loudly and sat down, regaining his composure. "Besides, intelligence shows that there aren't that many civilian casualties. Intelligence shows rather that entire villages are leaving before there is any incursion of human rights, to avoid the war altogether."

"You believe that?"

"Well, they are moving at night, that much we know, otherwise the satellites would see them during the day." His speech sped up. "This is typical refugee behaviour, which historically repeats itself."

"Then," Frank shrugged and paused for gravity, "where are they?"

Silence for a few moments.

"Frank. A few thousand people can redistribute themselves in a country this size, and we would never know the difference. They could move to Herzegovina or Croatia, for example, for any of a dozen different reasons. We'll never know." Richter looked like he might be convincing Frank.

The surgeon was searching his soul.

Finally he said, "I was in Rwanda, and it was just like this. People were assumed to be moving around under the cover of the jungle until hundreds of thousands of them turned up dead."

"Frank, that was Africa—This is Europe." He raised his eyebrows, and shrugged.

"No. This is the Balkans. Besides, in Rwanda, the UN general knew the killing was going on, but UN headquarters in New York didn't believe him either. You know what they did to him after he saved those thirty-seven thousand people in the stadium?"

"Yes." Richter studied his hands, folded in his lap.

"The problem here is that *your people aren't even looking!*" Frank got up and leaned on the desk, looking down at Richter. "Do you know whether they're using the infrared satellite at night, or are they just taking pictures during the day, the way they did in Africa?"

"You're pushing!"

"Well, do you know?" Frank slapped the desk.

Richter bolted upright, tipping his chair against the wall, and leaned forward. "I know what UNPROFOR tells me about the situation." He struck his chest once with his fist. "I am an officer serving in the United

Nations Protective Force, and I will tell you what you need to know, when you need to know it! You are still a civilian serving under my protection. You are not here to tell us how we police this unrest. *You have no authority.*"

"My point is that we're sitting here on this hilltop, where we're supposed to be helping the natives, but we're not. We're sitting here helping the UN, and that is why we're afraid of the natives." Richter glared. Frank crossed his hands against the coming protest. "We're afraid of the snipers because the locals think we're part of the main UN force. And don't tell me we're not." He turned sideways and gestured toward the widow covered with a tarpaulin. "Look!"

Richter looked like he knew he was losing. "A routine precaution."

"I've never seen this much cover anywhere!" Frank looked incredulous. "Even in Rwanda with the Hutus and the Tutsis dancing around us, infected with genocidal fever, they never looked at us sideways because they *knew* we were a humanitarian force."

"*Routine!*" Richter shouted and made a throwaway gesture with his right hand.

"Well, I can tell you that when I cross the square at night, I'm sure every tree, every bush, every rock out there has eyes." He was talking quickly. "Those eyes are rifle scopes, just like the alleyways of Sarajevo. And when the moon comes out…"

"We're well protected, Frank." Richter looked conciliatory. He came around the desk and put his hand on Frank's shoulder. "Our intelligence is good. In addition to our own men, we have Hradich, the Liaison."

"Are you sure about him?" Frank was calming.

"Sarajevo assigned him to us. I've seen his dossier. He's neutral. He's clean."

"How can anybody here be neutral?" Frank pleaded.

"This man has been guiding UN operatives for three years. His behaviour has never come under suspicion—and I tell you this privately, as a friend."

Frank shook his head slowly, wearily. "How can anybody here be neutral?"

"I grant you, in Sarajevo the factions are killing each other. Singly *und en masse*. All those people thrown together with no chance of escape—there comes mob mentality. Yes, there's sniper alley, where even old friends kill each other. But Frank, here in the country people are more dependent on each other. Religion means less, person to person. No mob effect. Sarajevo, yes. Here, no. Intelligence supports that. I'm sure."

"Kurt, I hope you're right." Frank sat back down, leaned forward and cradled his head in his hands. "I want my view reported officially." He looked up and considered the situation. "Forget the part about Hradich—but I don't think we should be doing UN soldiers."

Richter acknowledged the surgeon. "I will file your views officially with UNPROFOR in Sarajevo this afternoon. I will give you a copy. But I say again—we have no word of civilian casualties here."

Frank extended his hand, they shook, and he said, "Not yet."

He got up and walked to the door to let himself out. The door was partly open.

Colonel Richter said, "Frank…"

The surgeon turned back.

"Keep your shutters closed."

FIVE

Crack!

The door splintered open. The soldier covered the room with his gun. Three more blue helmets burst in with automatic weapons. They swept the room and ran to the side of the next door. On program, two of them went through the door together, guns levelled. The kitchen looked undisturbed. They checked two bedrooms off to either side. No sign. Cupboards. Closets. No entry to an attic. Warily, they scoured the floor and found the false door. One ripped it open, with three pointing their automatics into the black abyss. They threw in a torch and withdrew. Slowly they came back to the perimeter, weapons ready. A good look and the first one went down, followed by two others. Nothing. After a short while they came back out.

The entry to the attic was outside. A nearby ladder was raised. Same drill. No results. The building was clean.

Colonel Richter and Frank Lambert were standing by one of the troop carriers outside. Richter got a report and authorized another house. Three other NATO groups reported negative searches. Similarly, they went on.

Hradich said, "I take the church," and motioned one of his men to go along. "Make sure no snipers," he said to Richter, looking sideways as he strode by.

Church towers were a problem. They all knew that. One wild man could hold a whole town at bay and take out a significant percentage. Like in Sarajevo.

Frank already knew what that search would bring. Richter, on the other hand, was strictly military. It had to be done.

More negative reports from the other groups. One by one, Richter authorized more homes to be searched.

Frank visually assessed for himself the thirty-five or forty houses in the village, nestled in a nice valley by a river. The trees beyond the fields were green mixed growth. The situation was like Rwanda, yet so different. Almost home—so *civilised*.

This was Frank's third rescue mission since his posting to Yugoslavia. The searches hadn't found anybody before. He knew this mission wouldn't be different. All of his experience with these rescue missions conjured up only one impression. He knew!

And Hradich searching the church. Well, Frank had his thoughts… But then Richter trusted Hradich. So, Frank had to as well. But Hradich's talk on the way there, three hours of discourse on the beautiful country, villages, rivers, churches and bridges. And the negative impact of the UN. Tearing the country apart? Not furthering the national goal? Creating myths of ethnic cleansing?

What reasonable man could say such things under these circumstances? Frank had serious doubts!

More negative reports from the soldiers.

More orders. Search more houses.

Frank glanced back at the Med-Evac unit. There was Gwen. She nodded at him. He turned away and saw the dusty cobblestone road and the threatening sky.

Hradich came back with his man and reported that the church was clean.

Frank jammed his cold hands into his pockets and stared down. The road. The dust. Was it brown? He thought a moment. There wasn't any brown soil in Yugoslavia.

Richter caught him off guard. He said, "You see, everybody has left. It is like UNPROFOR reports." Like a teacher to a child, he held his arms out wide. "The people have all gone."

Frank thought in amazement, *How can he say that—and believe it?*

A crack of thunder. Then Frank thought he heard jets. He searched the sky—nothing.

UN soldiers were running up the streets to the convoy. Richter was speaking into his satellite phone. He pocketed it and shouted, "Everybody into the trucks." Then with urgency, *"Everybody into the trucks!"*

Frank caught a glimpse of Gwen pulling the tarpaulin down over the back of the Med-Evac. She saw him and motioned. *Hurry.*

Two jets shrieked over the village. American F-15 Eagles, fully loaded—Strike Eagles. Eight Canadian F-18s flew above, dressed with Sidewinders and what looked like other missiles under their wings.

"Duck!" shouted Richter.

The group obeyed.

Nothing happened.

Frank looked up to see the F-15s flying a wide circle between the hills. It started to rain hard. The F-18s had broken off into pairs overhead. Two of them seemed headed for a hillside. Then he saw smoke from under their wings, and the side of the hill erupted into impact points. There was a big bright flash in the centre of the impact area, and the reverberating boom reached them as the F-18s pulled away.

Richter shouted, "SAM site! Get in the van! Get in the van!"

The Yugoslavians' easily movable surface-to-air missiles had become a huge problem.

The jet noise was coming from everywhere, reverberating around the buildings. *Holy shit!* The F-15s were coming in from the side, just over trees on the other side of the town, not five hundred metres away.

"Hit the dirt," Frank shouted, not knowing if anybody else saw them.

Two deafening blasts tugged at clothing and whacked open the tarp at the back of the troop carrier. Fine debris and rocks pelted them and abraded exposed skin.

Just one more second. He had avoided the wave of burning heat by lying on the cobblestone. He picked himself up off the wet pavement and ran to the back of the truck, as the remains of two smoky fireballs drifted into the sky. A huge piece of rock thumped a dent into the cobblestone beside him. When he was in the truck, deafened, he shouted at Richter, "I thought we were coming to look for victims!"

"We were."

"No, we weren't. We came to clear the village!"

"The bridge is on a supply route the Bosnians are using to shell Sarajevo."

Sure. Frank pulled the tarp up to get a glimpse of the village as the convoy of three carriers departed.

The rain was heavy, plopping on the tarp cover of the carrier, so heavy he couldn't see the far end of the village. Water trickled over the cobblestone street, between the ghosts of stone houses, picking up the brown dust. But where the water pooled or flowed in gutters, *it flowed red.*

SIX

"Gwen, I tell you it was blood. The planes came—I got down flat—it was already raining. So water got on my fatigues. I tested it here with a hemastik. It was blood!"

They were sitting at a small white table in his quarters, lit by a single bulb.

"Didn't see it. Scared shitless by those planes. Couldn't look back." She shook her head. "No sir, not me. But seriously. Why do they always use such big bombs?"

He looked at her. "Those are the smallest they've got." Frank reached across the painted white table with the solitary lamp on it and held Gwen's hands firmly. He said, "You've got to back me on this. Let's do another hemastik, then we'll tell Richter…"

"Frank, I know where you're going with this. He won't change. Richter won't change his mind." She looked perplexed. "He's walking the party line…" her voice trailed off, "the UNPROFOR party line."

"He can't argue with a hemastik…"

"Sure he can." She squeezed his hands, thinking it was so simple, and turned away with a saddened expression. "I can too."

Frank was puzzled.

She said, "Accepting the fact that it was blood, how do you know it was human?"

"Pardon? Gwen, this is a war zone. Specifically, there's a genocide going on. Animals don't do genocide, people do."

"Frank, I believe it too, but UNPROFOR doesn't. They'll say that yes, there was blood, but the villagers had a market, slaughtered some cattle, some chickens, some sheep … something." She held her hand up to the coming protest. "And there's no way to confirm what kind of blood it is out here." She seemed confident that her logic had him good.

A soft knock at the door.

They turned toward it, startled, not expecting anyone.

Again, rap, rap, rap.

Frank went over, and his giant shadow followed him, contorted on the cupboards of the far wall. He opened the door.

"Hradich," he said, surprised. "Come in."

Stepping in out of the dark, the visitor said, "Best you keep close." His eyes darted between Frank and Gwen. "Could be sniper."

"Yes," said Frank. He closed the door tight. "What can I do for you?"

"Maybe we talk." Hradich's dark brown eyes perfectly set off the handlebar moustache on his craggy face, trying not to seem anxious, but again he looked at Gwen and then Frank. "Maybe we talk private?"

"I was going anyway." Gwen went for the door, and impassively let herself out.

Remembering the last couple of nights with her in bed, Frank was sorry to see her leave. He lingered with the memory for a moment, remembering the feel of her bare skin—her fine athletic form—but caught himself.

He swallowed hard, turned to Hradich and said, "Sure." He smiled at his guest. "Come in, sit down."

Hradich took the AK-47 off his shoulder and planted it beside a cupboard. His black beret went up the sleeve of his tunic when he placed it over the back of the chair, leaving his hair dishevelled.

"I don't have anything to offer you." Frank thought quickly and added, "Nothing to drink."

"Is okay, maybe we smoke."

"Sure." They lit a couple of cigarettes.

"I have problem."

"What kind of a problem?"

Hradich leaned forward slightly. "Serious problem I not can fix."

"What makes you think I can help?"

"You can. But if you want?"

"Even if I want to, there's only so much I can do." Frank studied his face. The bare bulb on the table gave up creases he hadn't seen before. Creases around the eyes. Creases of sorrow, or cruelty? "The problem is… medical?"

"Ya."

"You tell me what it is."

"You keep secret?" The curl of smoke from Hradich's cigarette played itself out in faint shadow on the far wall.

"If I can. But believe me, if I do anything around here, Colonel Richter will know." Frank felt sick for where this was going.

Hradich leaned further forward, rolling his cigarette nervously between his fingers, sizing Lambert up. The hard light glistened on his oily cheek. "Okay." He looked deep into Frank's eyes for a moment. "Problem not me. Is my girl, my daughter."

"All right."

"Nobody can know." Hradich appeared suddenly agitated. He pointed at Frank's face and said, "Until you say what you will do."

That caught Frank off guard. "You want me to keep this secret until I tell you what I think or decide?"

"Ya."

"I can do that."

"Okay." Hradich fumbled nervously, like a man on the brink. He studied Frank. His lips quivered. "Is my daughter." His head suddenly sank. "She have trouble."

Frank's jaw dropped a little. "You telling me what I think you're telling me?"

Uncontrollable tears welled in Hradich's eyes, and he blubbered, "She have big trouble."

"What kind of trouble?"

"Girl trouble." His head swayed from side to side. "She… *rape.*" Hradich began to cry uncontrollably and buried his face in his hands.

Frank reached across the table. Put his hand on his arm. Gave him a little shake. "That's okay, that's okay. You can tell me." Suddenly Frank had a lump in his throat and a lot of empathy for this man he had never really trusted. First, he had to get Hradich calmed down. That took some time, more than Frank would have guessed. When he finally looked up, this warrior with the AK-47, his eyes were bloodshot and tearful. Frank smiled reassuringly. "Hey, we can make anything better. But first things first. How old is your daughter?"

"Fourteen." Hradich began to cry into his arms again. As much as he might have wanted to, he couldn't control his emotions.

Holy shit, thought Frank. "Hradich! *Hradich!*" He shook him again. Hradich looked up with tears running down his face. "What's her name?"

"Zivka."

Frank thought a moment. "Zivka. What a beautiful name." He didn't even know Hradich had a family, much less a daughter. But why shouldn't he? And why shouldn't he keep her far away from this hellhole? Only now she had a problem of her own!

"She beautiful girl. She good girl. Now this…" He choked and began to cry again.

"Hradich. How long is she pregnant? Err, when did her bleeding stop?"

"Maybe month. Maybe two."

Typically reliable menstruation history, thought Frank. The bane of gynaecologists. "I'll have to examine her."

"You examine her like doctor, not like man?" Hradich was suddenly very composed, wielding his fingers toward Frank's face.

"Like a doctor," Frank agreed, "with Nurse Pakin."

"Good. You are friend." He started to fight back his tears, control the sobbing, like he hoped he hadn't lost too much face.

Maybe Frank had misjudged him all this time. He'd had his doubts. Maybe their cultures were just far enough apart that Frank got the message wrong. This was obviously a man with a lot of feeling—a family man with deep concerns, pride and humility like anybody else.

"Hradich. Who did this to her? Do you know?"

"What matter?"

"It does matter, Hradich. It does matter." He thought a moment. "Hradich, what's your first name?"

"Kamenko."

"All right, look, Kamenko…" He seemed much better. "I'll help *your* daughter in any way I can, but I definitely have to look at her first—I mean, examine her."

"With nurse, like doctor."

"Yes. But I have to know more. I have to know how this happened."

Hradich opened and closed his hands on the table as he looked down. "Not easy for me! I come here to help UN. Special advisor. Liaison. Now I ask for you help?"

"That's okay. I'll help you. We all will."

Hradich took a nervous drag of his cigarette and stabbed it out in a bowl.

The bowl clanked from side to side.

The Liaison went on. "How this happen? I not know. Not my people. Maybe Slovenians? Maybe Muslims?"

He seemed to become a little wary, perhaps wondering how many more questions he had to endure.

Frank said, "You're sure it's not a boy down the street?"

Hradich looked puzzled.

"A neighbour who sees your daughter every day? You know what I'm thinking, Kamenko?" He allowed himself the familiarity. "I'm thinking this sort of thing usually happens with people who know each other. People usually want someone they see every day, someone very close. Someone they can't have, and the next thing you know… rape. Sometimes murder. All kinds of abuse."

Hradich now looked at him rather incredulously.

"In my country the police always search very close to the scene of the crime, or it's random. You know what I mean?"

"No!" Hradich was sitting up, almost in protest. "My people not do this!"

"Okay. So let's think very carefully. Who would?"

"People some other village," he said quickly.

"Kamenko, do people from other villages come here often?"

"No."

"How about some soldiers from far away come to your village? See your daughter?"

"No!"

"What if they don't like your daughter? What if they don't like you?"

"Everybody here like me. I UN Liaison." He paused. "I good. I kind everybody!"

"Then why people from another village?"

Kamenko Hradich suddenly looked very sad, very disturbed. He almost spat, "Don't know!"

Frank felt the wall coming up. He couldn't figure out the disconnect. The impatience. He had been coached about this sort of thing. *In a foreign theatre, culturally misunderstood questions could get an inadvertent hostile response.* What part of this foreign theatre didn't Frank understand?

The neighbouring village? Soldiers passing through? The boy next door? War rape?

Frank thought he'd better not try deep waters. "Kamenko," he said, leaning forward and putting both his hands firmly on Hradich's shoulders, "I'll see your daughter tomorrow at 1100 hours in the clinic. With Nurse Pakin. I promise everything will be okay."

At first it was uneasy, just a hint of a curl at the corners of his mouth. Slowly, Hradich's smile hardened into a look of satisfaction.

SEVEN

The young girl squirmed under the white sheet. Gwen had gotten her undressed and stood on her left. Zivka had layers of long black hair that flowed over the edges of the gurney. Her eyes were dark brown, dominated by finely arched brows. Her lips, a healthy red, were offset by cherubic cheeks. Unpainted hands tucked the sheet up to her neck. The examining area was surrounded by white curtains.

Frank put his hand on her belly.

"Ah!" she cried.

The main door cracked open.

"Zivka." Panic in Hradich's voice. "*Sve uredu?*" (Are you okay?)

"*Da, Tata!*" (Yes, Papa.)

"The nurse is there?"

"Everything's okay here, Kamenko. I'm going to examine your daughter in a moment, with Nurse Pakin." Frank could almost see the pained expression on daddy's face. "I promise I'll take good care of her."

There was a pause. "Okay. Okay… you are friend."

The door creaked closed.

The surgeon turned to Zivka. "I'm going to examine you now, sweetheart. Nothing to worry about. Put your legs up like this." He manoeuvred the ankles together with the knees pointing up forty-five degrees. "There. Now hold Nurse Pakin's hands."

She did.

"And take a few deep breaths."

Gwen pursed her lips and breathed deeply in and out, holding Zivka's hands closely, until the teenager followed suit. Finally, breathing rhythmically, the young girl gazed at the ceiling with a look of abandon.

Frank drew her knees apart and raised the sheet up onto her belly.

Not the sort of thing he usually did, but he had done a few of these exams before. Prior to emergency surgery. He knew he could pull it off reliably.

Frank gloved his hands and lubricated his index and middle fingers. With his left hand on her belly, he entered her vagina with his right index finger. It passed easily. No hymen. Not a virgin. *Of course not, she had been raped.* He went in farther, and the tip of his finger slid past the small cervix and onto the uterus. He traced out a shape about the size of a small orange. Frank glanced at Gwen, who returned a barely perceptible nod. He withdrew his hand and went back with his index and middle fingers. He confirmed the size of an orange between his two fingers and his hand on the belly. Surprisingly, Zivka didn't stir. He felt out to each side and didn't find masses around the ovaries. He looked at Zivka blowing, concentrating on the ceiling. Her hands grasping the edge of the sheet gave away their secret, dirt under her fingernails. Frank withdrew.

He threw away the gloves. "I'm going to see your Papa. You were a good girl." He squeezed her right hand. "Nurse Pakin is going to take care of you now—Get you dressed." He turned to Gwen . "All right?"

She smiled at Zivka and wrinkled her nose. "Sure."

Frank let himself out of the examining area and walked across the makeshift operating room to the main door. He went through, and Hradich sprang to his feet from the chair beside the duty sergeant.

"Yes?"

"We need to talk. In my room." He turned to walk out.

"We can talk outside," said Hradich. "No snipers. I see good!"

Frank looked back. That thing went through the back of his mind again. That fleeting thing—the temporary suspension of disbelief. Then he thought of Richter's words about the Liaison. And his own thoughts the night before. Frank corrected his logic but stood firm. "In my room!" He strode out, wearing nothing but his greens.

Frank heard Hradich's shuffling footsteps follow him across the square and enter his room. The door closed gently before he turned around. Hradich had his black beret in his trembling hand and was putting down his AK-47.

"You were right, Kamenko, your daughter has a problem." He waited a few seconds. "She's pregnant."

Hradich started slowly, almost imperceptibly to sob. His eyes moistened and his mouth gaped as he strengthened his shaking grip on his beret.

"She's about eight weeks pregnant." The surgeon in him let it settle in. "What are we going to do?"

Hradich arched his back and shrieked like an animal raising its hackles. He raised his hands and threw his beret at the floor. He stamped on it, then cried openly into his hands, covering his face.

Frank went over and held him. "It's all right, Kamenko, it's all right." He gripped the trembling man tighter.

The door creaked open. Two blue helmets with side arms peered in suspiciously.

"It's okay. Everything's okay." Frank held up his hands.

"We heard a loud noise, *sir!*"

"The Liaison is upset." He looked at Hradich for the soldiers. "Had some bad news. I'm helping him through it." He put his arms back on Hradich.

It took them a moment. "Yes, sir!" They pulled the door shut.

As Hradich wept, Frank's first thought was that Richter would hear about it. He would hear about the girl being examined. That much was to be expected. But he would also hear about this. There were going to be questions.

Hradich was regaining control. Frank let him go, and he started to pace.

"Kamenko, what are we going to do? What does Zivka want to do? Does she want to keep the baby?"

Hradich shot him a glance.

"Did you talk to her? Do you know what she wants to do?"

"I talk." He had a distant look about him. A disgusted look. "She not want baby."

"Are you sure?"

"Ya!" He paced like a caged tiger.

"Then what will we do?"

"You fix? You fix for me?" He stopped, and with a look of pleading said, "You fix for Zivka?"

Frank said, "You mean do an abortion?" Hradich looked at him like he didn't understand. "You mean take the baby out?"

"Ya."

Frank's heart sank. "Kamenko, I don't do that sort of thing, I'm a surgeon..."

"You good doctor. Can do."

He couldn't believe what he was hearing. And he couldn't believe where this was going. "I have to think about this. We're going to have to talk to Zivka and make sure that's what she wants. And then I'm going to have to talk to the colonel."

Damn.

EIGHT

"Help me. Help me—I'm dying."

Frank watched as the man, perhaps thirty or thirty-five, was dragged past by the intern and a nurse. A flurry of activity followed him to a stretcher in the empty treatment room.

"You've got to help me!" He sat clutching his chest as he looked up at the ceiling, breathing heavily.

"You're all right, sir. Relax. Sit back." The nurse helped him recline onto the head of a half-raised gurney.

The intern asked, "Do you have chest pain?"

"No!" The delirious man was swaying, trying to sit up. "Can't you see I'm dying!" he insisted, clawing at his chest.

"Sir, try to relax." The intern pushed him back down onto the stretcher. "Monitor leads. IV D-5-W stat! Cardiac pack stat."

A nurse fumbled with his arm. "I don't see any veins!"

Dr. Prosser, the senior emergency doctor, came in. "What's going on?"

Frank moved closer.

The intern said, "Came in off the street. No history. Says he's dying. Clutching his chest. That's it!"

A woman in a dress entered the room and said, "Medical records negative," and left.

"B.P. sixty over twenty-two," said a nurse. "Pulse one hundred and sixty."

"Get an IV in!" Prosser commanded. He put his stethoscope to the man's chest.

"Help me! Help me!" Squirming.

"Hold still please, sir." Prosser steadied the man's chest with his hand.

"You're choking me. You're choking me."

"I can't get an IV in," came from the far side of the gurney.

"O2 sats sixty percent," from another nurse.

"O2 mask one hundred percent." Prosser turned to Frank. "I need you."

Frank went to the head of the bed. He thought he saw the jugular vein. "Number twelve IV catheter." He doused the neck with alcohol. A nurse handed him the small plastic catheter with the steel core and steadied the man's head, exposing the right side of his neck.

"Don't choke me. Don't choke me." Squirming. Crying. "Help me!"

"Monitor shows flat complexes. Rate one hundred and seventy."

Frank pushed the sharp end of the catheter into the neck. He thought he had the jugular. No back flow. He threw the catheter into a basin. "Another number twelve."

"Help me." The man was whimpering. Shaking.

The nurse handed Frank the catheter and steadied the man's head.

"Help me. You're choking me!"

Frank felt his heart jump. He carefully entered the neck with the catheter.

The man cried out.

The nurse steadied him.

Frank carefully advanced the catheter. A bead of dark blue blood formed at the outside end of the catheter. "I've got it!" He attached the IV line.

The man became silent.

Prosser was shouting some orders for medication, when Frank looked up and saw him. A little boy. A frightened little boy in pajamas, standing alone on the other side of the room, hugging a teddy bear.

Frank's heart sped—he felt nauseated. "Who is that?" He pointed.

The intern said, "Walked in behind the patient."

Frank said, "Get him out of here."

The man had his arm up. He mouthed, "Help me. I'm dying."

"ECG's flat."

"Shock him, three hundred," said Prosser.

The machine beeped ready.

A nurse applied the paddles and delivered the shock. Nothing. The ECG stayed flat.

"Three hundred again. Quick two amps of bicarb."

The machine signalled ready. Then—whack!

Nothing changed.

Prosser said, "Has to be tamponade." He turned to Frank. "Open him up."

Frank approached the table from the right. He spilled hibitane all over the chest and abdomen. He was gowned and put on sterile gloves.

Tension bristled his neck.

A tray was thrown open and he took the scalpel. The nurse doing CPR withdrew. Frank made a large deep cut across the abdomen, under the ribs. He put one hand in and with the other inserted a clamp, which he opened repeatedly until he got through the diaphragm. Grey-blue blood welled up and over the sides of the body, spilling onto the floor. Frank's feet were soaked with it.

"Complete asystole. I'm massaging him." He felt the perspiration on his back.

"Pour in the fluid," said Prosser.

Frank looked past Prosser, past the patient's feet and saw him again—the little boy. Standing there with his mouth open. The teddy dangling from his right hand. The little boy looked up, right at Frank. Like he saw through him. In a trance.

Frank's heart pounded—stopped—and pounded—and choked him. He clutched his chest, smearing himself with dusky blood. His chest was heaving. He tore at his chest.

Prosser was looking at him—coming to him—reaching for his shoulder. His voice was fading, fading away. Prosser's image was dissolving into the surroundings. Like he was being beamed to another world.

He felt the rubbing on his shoulder.

"Frank. Frank." A woman.

He had clutched his chest with both arms—holding his coffee mug tight to his chest. So tight that the woman couldn't pry it loose.

Coffee had spilled onto his shirt.

"Frank. Frank. What's wrong?"

He looked over and saw a black woman with short straight hair. It took a moment before he slowed down his breathing and realized it was Gwen.

"It's okay," she said. "You're okay, Frank." She paused a moment and said, "What happened to you?"

Frank looked at her as he relaxed his arms and put the mug on the table. He looked down at his shirt, wet with spilled coffee, and looked around.

Gwen was sitting opposite him at the breakfast table. Dayna was standing behind her, eyes agog.

He had no idea what they had just witnessed, but from their expressions, it must have been bad.

He looked up at Dayna and mouthed, "It's okay," without saying it.

She went back behind the counter.

There was nobody else in the cafeteria. He was thankful for that.

***

Gwen leaned close across the table and said, "Where were you just now?"

He shook his head and said, "I don't know."

From the moment he had started to stare at the far wall, a partition of shaved timbers with nothing to distract him, she knew. She had turned to check behind her, just in case, but saw nothing. Then his rapid breathing that almost turned to hyper-ventilation—and clutching the coffee mug. The whole thing had only lasted about fifteen seconds, but seemed much longer.

She had heard of this sort of thing, but had never seen it before.

Surveying his shirt, wet with spilled coffee that he never felt. Looking in his eyes, she saw a look of horror, still.

Gwen wondered what secrets hid inside him. Far behind the conscious, behind the deepest reach?

She took his hands in hers and rubbed her thumbs across his knuckles. Her eyes were wide with worry, when she said, "We need to get you some help."

Frank shot her an incredulous look, and said, "I'll be all right."

NINE

"You want to do what?"

"A simple D&C."

"That's an abortion," said Richter.

"Well. Actually. Yes."

"On Hradich's daughter?"

"Yes."

"What's the matter with your head?" He pointed at his temple and tapped it twice. "What are you thinking?" Richter sounded pressured. "We're running a humanitarian mission here, not an abortion clinic!"

"It's just one case. For Kamenko and his daughter." Frank thought for a moment—thought like an American ought to. "We have to do what we can for our own." *That's a bit weak.* "For our allies." He felt sheepish. "Just like us."

Richter was sitting behind his big desk, looking at him like he had two heads. His blond eyebrows scowled a perfect chevron.

Frank knew he hadn't reached a single ounce of Teutonic logic.

"Well, that's just the way it is. War, I mean. Shit happens to people you like. What makes a difference is what we do about it. Like any civilized nation."

Richter's face was like a stone.

A few long minutes went by. Richter didn't stir. Frank was beginning to rethink his position.

Richter must have realized the validity of the argument. If Hradich had gone to Frank Lambert and asked him for help ... and if Richter said *No* to a request for help from his Liaison... one that Frank had already agreed to... well... he was in a corner.

Richter's stone face finally relaxed, and he said, "If we go ahead with this, and I say *if*, what am I going to report to my superiors?"

Frank breathed a sigh of relief. "You tell them we aborted your Liaison's daughter, whose rape was an act of war. Simple. Tell the truth."

"This is some kind of first!"

"Well, it may be for the UN, but it isn't for relief workers. I can assure you of that."

"Really?" Richter looked distraught.

"Oh, come on. We both know that rape is a time-honoured act of war. What's different is that we're doing something about it."

"You have to promise me you'll be frugal with our resources." He shook a finger.

Frank shrugged and put his hands in his pockets. "Come on, Kurt. You're thinking this way because this isn't a battlefield casualty. Nobody's shot—or wounded. This girl's been hurt in a way she'll feel for the rest of her life." He came around the big desk and put his hand on Richter's shoulder. "This is where we show some compassion."

"All right. All right." Richter waved the surgeon's hand off his shoulder. "You can do it. And tell Hradich the colonel will do whatever it takes to help and protect his Liaison's family."

"I would have said that anyway."

Richter looked at him, dolefully. "I know."

Frank slowly backed away, gave a casual salute, and walked out of the heavily curtained office.

Outside he ran into Hradich.

"Yes?" His eyes pleaded.

Frank said, "All right. We can do … uh … operate on your daughter."

"So you fix?"

"Come here." Frank pulled Hradich around the side of the administrative building, out of earshot, into the shadows and said, "This is going to be hard on Richter. He's never approved anything like this before." Hradich nodded, and Frank continued, "And I've never done anything like this before."

"You fix!" Hradich nodded rapidly and smiled.

"Kamenko." Frank thought he needed to be up close and honest—more like in his face. "This operation isn't without risk…" Hradich seemed bewildered. Wasn't he getting it? "This operation could hurt Zivka." Still a look of disbelief. "Something could go wrong." He began to wave circles with his right hand. "Could make mistake!"

"No!" Hradich smiled broadly. "You good friend." He nodded. "You fix good!"

Oh Christ! Frank said, "You need to do something for me."

Hradich continued to smile and nod approval. "Anything. You name."

"I need a willow bough." Hradich looked baffled again. "I need a big branch from a willow tree. A very dry willow tree."

Hradich said, "I find. I get." He smiled again and pounded his chest twice with his right hand. "I fix!"

TEN

Frank had the willow bough. Hradich had dropped it off earlier in the morning. It was a beauty. Thick. Dry. Well barked, with no splits. Absolutely no sign of rot. Hradich had kept his promise. Frank spent all day whittling it into pointy cones. Every time he finished one, about half a centimetre wide and four to five centimetres long, he thought he could do better. By three in the afternoon, he had quite a collection, and he had high hopes for them.

He was sitting on a bench, legs crossed, between his building and the next in a narrow alleyway. The sun had come and gone. In deep shadows, he was getting cold and starting to shiver. The bench, his feet and the ground were littered with wood shavings. He gathered up his cones into a Ziploc bag.

At noon, he had put one cone into a water glass in his room. It got too cold to continue working outside by late afternoon. He decided it was time to check on his test, and went inside.

He held up the glass, shook it and smiled at the fattened piece of wood. Couldn't believe his eyes. The piece was marginally longer than it had been but at least three times as wide—well, maybe he would believe his eyes. He put the glass down and fished out the cone. Rolling it between his fingertips, he confirmed his feelings. He smiled, felt an inner warmth, and flashed through thoughts of an old friend who had told him about this.

Frank was feeling confident, starting to chuckle, thinking he was going to pull it off. Archaic technology or not, he was going to pull it off! But he needed to do another test before he could be sure. Frank needed to sterilize a cone. Trouble was, he was getting hungry. Oh well. He'd tell Gwen to meet him, and they'd stop at the canteen afterward.

Gwen had the autoclave up and running in no time. It was in the corner of the casualty room.

"I don't get this!" she said as she eyed Frank, clearly bewildered. "You want to sterilize a piece of wood?"

"Yeah." He threw the word away, looking at the far wall.

"Whatever for?"

"Well, you see, dry willow has fabulous potential for expansion when it gets wet." He pulled the plastic bag out of his fatigue's pocket. "I have to know that it won't expand in the autoclave." He pulled out a cone.

Gwen's eyes widened as she took the bag of cones. "You've lost me completely, Frank. Or you're completely lost. Why are we doing this?"

"Oh, I thought you knew?"

"No. Explain."

"In the old days, I'd say in the seventies, doctors used this technique to do abortions. The girl came to the clinic the night before, and one of these—they're called tents—got slipped into her cervix."

"Slipped?" She shook her head in disapproval.

"Well, placed. You know. With a spec, like at a pap smear. Then the girl goes to sleep for the night, and the next morning her cervix is all dilated with the tent. The doctor pulls it out and does a painless abortion."

"Why don't you just put her to sleep, dilate her up and do an abortion like in the States or any other civilized country?"

"Here's the brilliant part." Frank didn't realize he was beaming. "This works just as well. *And* we don't use any excess drugs, which would piss Richter off." He dug into the Ziploc he was holding and proudly handed Gwen a tent.

She looked at it and then at him with displeasure. She placed it into a shallow metal tray, which went into the autoclave, and locked it tight. She made a few adjustments to the controls and said, "Where did you learn this alchemy?"

"Had a friend when I was a resident in Boston. French guy named Claude Savigny. We were really close. He was full of stories about how things used to be done and where they were going."

"So here you were a little woodworker today, and you carved all these tents. All for one girl?"

Her sarcasm cut. He decided to admit to that, "Actually it was kind of fun, and after a while I just tried to carve better cones."

She stared at him. Blank. Like she understood his logic but still wondered if he wasn't coming a little undone.

Frank shrugged. "Want to get a snack?"

Over at the canteen, Dayna was getting things ready for supper.

"Mind if we graze?"

"Go ahead," she said with a heavy Southern accent. "Make yourselves at home."

He saw her look back at him, a double take, as if to make sure he was all right.

Then Frank noticed Dayna's smile dissolve again the moment Jennifer walked into the cafeteria.

Strange. Why does Dayna do that? He couldn't remember a single time she had chastised her helper.

Gwen was fast, in behind the counter, and into a large fridge. A modern stainless steel fridge that was out of place in this room with bare boards on the ceiling, exposed under raw timber framing. She was onto a slice of cold pizza, and Frank, right behind her, got a chicken drumstick.

"Evening." The large wooden door thudded closed behind Father John. He came up to the other side of the counter and looked from one to the other. "Getting a little extra, are we?" He nodded broadly. "Getting ready to burn the midnight oil?"

"Just a little snack, Father." Gwen shook her head. "Nothing since breakfast!"

"And Doctor Lambert…?"

Frank caught the formality, and it stuck to him. What had happened to Frank and John?

Finally, Father John said, "I understand you are going to do an abortion on Hradich's daughter?"

"That's right."

Gwen watched carefully but instinctively moved offside as she nibbled her pizza.

"Hmm…" Father John exhaled as he barely shook his head. "That's not how God treats His children!"

"Oh no?" said Frank. "And how does God treat *His* children?" Somehow, he thought that *this* priest had no right to talk about the treatment of children. Although he didn't know why.

Father reached for a cup and said, "He treats them all equally, Doctor."

"Oh. So, He causes His violated children to bear the unwanted fruit of war?"

"God's children are all equal before Him. And besides, there's no war going on around here." Confident. "I think we all know that." Father John turned to Gwen and to Dayna.

Father John may as well have had Colonel Richter's head bolted onto his shoulders. Frank knew that much. He came around the counter, still working on the drumstick, to face Father John. "But there is a war going on. There's a genocide. I can smell it. I can see it when the streets run red after rains in deserted villages. Those people didn't leave! They were exterminated. Soon this genocide will even wake you up! And when you do, what will you tell the people? The ones that are still alive carrying the scars and burdens, the spoils and rape of war. What will you tell them?" He waited a moment to regain control, starting to loathe the pious face of Father John. "That God considers them equal? Go ahead, forgive each other and bear the fruit of war. Believe me, Father, when this is all over, the dead will be the lucky ones."

"I can see you're not in the mood to listen—"

"Not in the mood?" Frank cut in, starting to seethe with anger. "I've listened to this sort of shit before! In Rwanda, nearly a million people slaughtered each other. I was there. Nobody, but nobody paid any attention to that genocide. Not the UN. No aid agency. Not any church." A tear welled up in his left eye. "Nobody but that damned Canadian General, and the troops and officers who served under him. When they got 'cease and desist' orders, they took thirty-seven thousand people who would have been killed and guarded them in a fucking ball field. *A ball field!*" He poked his bare drumstick at Father John's fatigues. "You know what they got for saving those people?" He calmed down a moment. "Court martialled! All of them!"

"Your point?"

"My point is, God doesn't help the victims or the victors of war, and He doesn't help those who intervene. Ignoring the issue is your personal choice. I hope you can live with yours. I *know* I can live with mine!" Frank stared down Father John.

Father fumbled his cup onto the counter with a clatter, turned around and went for the door. It slammed shut behind him.

Gwen, seeing Frank's agitation, came up and put her hand around his waist.

Dayna came around, actually carrying some food to a table, set it, put down some hot coffees and gestured with her open black arms. "Well, sit down and eat."

They did. They sat there for the longest time without saying anything.

Finally, Gwen said, "You see what's happening?" She put her hands on his and squeezed lightly.

"Won't be easy, but I'm standing firm," said Frank.

"I know, and I respect that." She squeezed his hands again. "Just watch your back."

They ate the last of the pizza and chicken, and drained the coffees.

Gwen checked her watch. "Time's up for the autoclave."

They got up and went for the door.

"'Night, Dayna." Gwen waved.

Frank said, "Thanks," walking backward.

"Y'all keep your chin up," Dayna said, holding her cup high in salute, standing there, looking as wide as she was tall, in her big stained apron. Every inch a southern girl.

"We will," they answered in unison.

A few moments later they were in the casualty room. The light on the autoclave was green. The cycle was over.

Gwen broke the seal. A bit of steam hissed out. She took a green surgical towel and pulled out the dish.

They peered in. The tent rolled on the floor of the pan, looking no larger than when it had gone in. Smooth. Crisp. Clean! They smiled at each other.

Frank said, "Hallelujah!"

ELEVEN

Zivka had come with her father the night before the operation. Gwen made sure the girl had eaten before arriving. She gave her an injection.

Hradich wanted to know the reason for everything. "What you give?"

"Some Gravol so her stomach won't get upset," Gwen had told him.

"Why should get upset?"

"She's going to have an operation," Frank said.

"Tomorrow!"

"Yes, but I have to get her ready tonight."

"But…"

Frank put his arm around the father's shoulder. "Kamenko, do you trust me or not?"

A moment, and Hradich said, "I trust." He paused. Softly, "I trust."

"Then let us do our job. We'll give Zivka back to you, good as new." Hradich didn't answer quickly, and Frank knew that Zivka would never be good as new to her father. He sighed.

Hradich finally said, "Is good," with the resignation of a desperate parent giving up their child to the care of a stranger.

A giant leap of trust Frank had seen countless times before. An injured loved one left in his operating room for him to work his magic. If he could get his genie out of the bottle. And sometimes he couldn't. That was the inherent risk. But for now, *is good,* was all the surgeon in him needed.

The rest of the night had been straightforward. Hradich finally left to meet Richter. That gave Frank and Gwen the opportunity to get the girl gowned and onto a gurney. Again, the black lines under the fingernails clutching the sheet. The latent signs of childhood, a childhood violated and gone now—forever.

Frank did what he had to. Legs up. Knees apart. Sheet up to the belly. Move in a light from below while Gwen soothed Zivka. In went the speculum. A gasp as he spread the spoons. Soothing words above.

Frank rocked the speculum until the cervix popped into sight. Long and grey, with a pinkish fringe in the harsh light, and a thick mucous plug in the entry hole. Pregnant.

There, with that little mucous plug, went all the delusions of childhood.

Then Frank took a narrow wood "tent" off the tray and manoeuvred the pointy end up the entry. He applied some gentle pressure, and it slowly slid in until the crown of the thick end was all that stuck out. All that with hardly a protest.

A while later they gave the girl some Valium, and finally Gwen bunked next to her in the recovery room.

He thought now, as he sat on the ledge in his darkened room, smoking a cigarette, about how he was going to take an unborn life tomorrow. Rob it of everything. But he was going to give Zivka back her life. He knew that.

And Hradich, well, he was doing this for him too. They were getting closer through this ordeal. That much was also certain. But that often happened at times like this.

And how easy the decision had been. Daddy had made it. Not like in the States. What does the girl want? No. No emotion. No baby coming that's half yours and half the enemy's. No confusion between love, hate and guilt. All that would be gone, with surgical precision.

TWELVE

Frank had slept soundly that night and now looked at Zivka, who was cowering under the blue drape of the gurney. Gwen had given her a shot of Versed to settle her, and Frank unloaded some Ketamine into the IV. Soon the patient was in another place, and Gwen draped and prepped her.

Frank inserted the speculum without any resistance after he spread her legs. The tent was in her cervix in full bloom, swollen to three times its former size. He pulled the willow piece out and proceeded to curette the sides of her uterus. Then the suction went in and the glass suction bottle in the corner of the makeshift operating room splashed red and hissed with the surrender of the remnants of a lost life.

Frank stared at the glass jar for a long moment. Then he scraped and suctioned again.

Still no protest from the patient.

Finally, he said to Gwen, "I think we're done here."

He removed the speculum and lowered Zivka's legs after placing a pad. He pulled up the blue drape, covering her, and observed her a moment. Her peaceful breathing raised and lowered the blue cover.

Gwen said, "I'll take care of everything."

"And I'll go talk to Papa."

Outside, Hradich followed him closely across the square. "Zivka is okay?"

"Yes. She's fine."

"You fix?"

Frank stopped and glanced back at him. "Yes, I fix." He continued walking to his quarters.

"I go see."

Frank turned around again. "Kamenko." He drew his shoulders back and exhaled. "You let her sleep a while."

"Is okay?"

"I said she's okay. Don't you trust me?"

"Yah, yah. I trust." Hradich surveyed Frank's face, almost like he was sizing him up. "I need talk."

"What about?"

"Maybe we talk private." He let his gaze drift to Frank's quarters.

"I see." He drew a deep breath again and let it go. "Come on then."

They walked across the square into Frank's room. He opened the shutters to let in a little light and sat down at the small white table.

Hradich took the AK-47 off his shoulder and propped it by the door.

Why does he always bring that damn gun?

Hradich walked over to the table and reached inside his oversize coat.

Frank felt a brief panic, but then he resigned all his fears.

Hradich pulled out a bottle of slivovitz.

"Kamenko…"

He held up his hand and said, "I bring you present for help Zivka." He placed it on the table.

"Kamenko, you don't have to do this."

"Quiet." Like it was an order. "You not drink with me?"

"Sure, I'll drink with you."

Frank got up, the two men embraced, and Hradich slapped him on the back—then he hugged him—hard. They sat down with a couple of glasses, and Hradich poured an inch of the prune brandy into each of the glasses.

They cheered, "*Salut*," and touched glasses.

Frank said, "To Zivka."

A smile came over Hradich, and he drained the glass.

The brandy had a fruity sweetness that made it appealing, but Frank reminded himself that he still had a patient post-op.

Hradich said, "You like?"

"Very much." Frank nodded. "So what's on your mind?"

"Is hard for me to say. But you good friend. Maybe you can fix?"

Feeling a little uneasy, Frank said, "What exactly do you want me to do?"

Hradich stared intently at Frank and said, "More girls like Zivka. Maybe you help?"

"What..."

THIRTEEN

"And when did she go home?" Richter eyed him with a satisfied smile. Almost like the thing had been his idea.

"We let her go this morning. Gwen and I decided to observe her for the night, because we're not used to doing these. So, just in case." Frank shrugged.

"I see." The smile faded. "You work well together. You consult."

He must know about us.

"We have different areas of expertise. Gwen's done a lot of gynaecology."

"Of course. And that is the modern way." Richter leaned back in his creaky oak rocker. "And I am glad that we finally have this behind us. Now we can concentrate on other things."

Frank sat down on the leather armchair and said, "Like, what other things? It's not as if the locals are showing up here with other problems." He leaned forward.

Richter's expression changed completely. He moved forward, propping his elbows on his desk, and said, "Are you trying to tell me something?"

He had that knowing expression on his face.

"Actually, I am." Frank swallowed hard.

Richter seemed to have noticed that.

"Hradich says there are more raped girls who need procedures."

"What?" Richter waved his right arm through the air in one incredulous gesture.

"I said…"

"I know what you said. You mean, there are more girls who want abortions."

"Well, as we agreed with Zivka, these are casualties of war, and we need to do the right thing for them. Don't you agree?" He paused a moment. "You agree. Don't you?"

Richter opened a drawer on his desk and pulled out a bottle of brandy and a glass. He poured himself a healthy inch, staring at the desktop.

"Hey, what about me," said Frank.

Richter pulled out another glass and slid it and the bottle across the desktop. Then he drained his glass.

Frank poured himself some and slid the bottle back to Richter, who poured himself another one. And a half.

Frank said, "Why so glum? At least we're helping these people. Besides, how could we do the UN Liaison's daughter and not do the other girls?" He looked around the room. "Maybe they're her friends."

"You know, Frank," Richter pronounced the A short, "I've been worried about this since I authorized Zivka. Err ... Hradich's daughter."

"Why?"

"I wasn't sure." He tapped the desktop. "But now I know."

"And?"

"I was worried it would turn into a cascade, like this." He thought a moment. "You know, there are NATO colonels who are leading assault groups in this conflict, down in Sarajevo. There's even one who is in charge of the aircraft. F-15s and F-18s. Nice airplanes!"

"And..."

"And I am stuck here in Bosnia, commanding your abortion clinic." Richter gazed at the ceiling. "*Ach du lieber.* I will never live this down."

"Why?"

Richter leaned farther forward, a fresh pour of brandy in his glass. "So how many more girls are there?"

"A few."

***

Frank watched Gwen getting undressed like he had before. She was slender and tall. Her black skin glistened with the highlights of the sole, dim light bulb. He noticed her breasts as she bent down to turn off the light.

She slid in under the cover, and he took comfort in her warmth. She began to rub his stomach with her left hand.

"So how many more girls are there? Did Hradich say?" said Gwen.

"Not really. He left me with the impression of ten to fifteen."

"I mean, how many can there be?"

Frank turned to her, looking at her head, propped on her right hand. "In a war, many."

"Not like the steady stream we'd get back home."

"No. Anyway, I'll clear that up with him tomorrow." He waited a moment. "You okay with this?"

"Doesn't bother me any. I figure whatever we can do for these girls, we need to do. Otherwise we're just sitting here on this hilltop waiting, for what?" She shrugged.

"Exactly. Now, there's one other thing I didn't tell you about Richter."

"Uh-huh?"

"I think he knows about us," said Frank.

"Of course he does. Are you daft?" Gwen poked him in the ribs. "He's the C.O. He's supposed to know."

"Yeah, but you were in the army, and I was in the air force..."

"Honey, honey. Chief operative words—was and were. We're not subject to those rules any more. So don't you start to loose your cool about that."

She let her hand slip down and began to rub him.. He quickly got hard.

"Want to play a game?" said Gwen. "It's duty calls."

She took his hand as she spread her legs and started him stroking her.

She was ready.

"This girl needs some *service*, Major."

Frank rolled on top and entered her, revelling in her smooth warmth. He started to stroke in and out.

She wrapped her arms around his neck and breathed rhythmically into his ear, getting into synchrony with him.

Frank got lost in the excitement and thrust faster. Realizing he was getting ahead of her, he slowed down, letting her catch up with every push.

Her breathing turned to sighs. More and louder. Until it became heavier. Then he pushed slowly faster, and harder. And faster.

Gwen clutched tighter. Her sighs deepened and finally she quivered and softly murmured in his ear, "Oh … oh … oh…"

Frank slowed down, just keeping her going.

Gwen unlocked her hold. She smiled a long moment, and then her expression became serious. She pushed him gently onto his back and got on top. She guided him back in and rocked back and forth. Slowly at first and then faster, and harder.

"Come on, baby," she purred, "fill me up."

Frank luxuriated in her thrusts. He massaged her buttocks as she kept her hands on her hips.

He marvelled at her black glistening skin. Then he felt his loins quiver as he came in a long, slow groan.

Gwen broke into a broad smile. "There. That's better."

With Frank still inside, she rotated to the left and they rolled on their sides. He closed his arms around her, and they drifted quickly into a deep sleep.

FOURTEEN

Hradich showed up like he said he would.

Before that, Frank had finished lunch with Gwen and Richter in the ramshackle building with part of a roof that they called the canteen.

Frank noted the colonel making eye contact with Jennifer, when she topped up the coffees. His lids opening wide...

She turned away without missing a beat.

Richter, said, "What are we going to do with these, these *children?*" He looked down-trodden. Like nobody would ever salute him again.

Frank told him that these were young women who were victims of war rape, believing that Richter would eventually get over it. He had to. Last week Richter, had committed to fifteen more girls. And Frank was afraid that was only the beginning. But with Hradich in the room, it was like the colonel didn't know how to say no. So the plan was that Hradich would bring five girls on Monday afternoon, and they'd get home on Wednesday. Five more on Thursday, and they'd get home on Saturday. And then again next Monday.

The crazy part that Frank didn't get, was that he was already looking forward to it. When he heard the truck and looked at his watch, he almost got up with a lick.

Right on time.

Hradich pulled up in a cloud of dust, driving a small pickup with a man beside him. In the back were five girls.

Hradich got out and motioned to the other man, who was getting out. "Is Branko Dinnich."

"Glad to meet you," said Frank as he shook his hand.

"*Dobro. Hvala.*"

Frank looked at the man who had gazed askance. Obviously younger than Hradich, but craggy nevertheless, with black hair and moustache. Same sort of well used adventure clothing—not military. At least no AK-47, unlike Hradich, who had laid his on the hood of his truck.

The man named Dinnich had gone to the back of the truck and let the tailgate down. He gave one girl a hand to get out.

Like him, she had black hair, straight and long to the shoulders. She was dressed like an Italian grandma. All in black.

Dinnich said, "Is my daughter, Vaida." He looked at her and then put his finger under her downturned face, causing her to look up. "Say hallo to doctor."

She raised her head for the slightest moment and said, "Hallo." When her sad brown eyes met Frank's, she immediately dropped her gaze again.

Frank put his hand on her shoulder and said, "Hello, Vaida. I'm Doctor Lambert." When she didn't respond, he gave her shoulder a little squeeze and let go.

Gwen had the other four girls, and she shook her head at Frank.

As they walked by, only one of the girls met his eyes and said, "Hallo."

Frank said, "Hello, girls. Welcome to my clinic," as cheerfully as he could.

Gwen directed them over to the general quarters building.

That was when Frank noticed Richter, a short distance away, leaning against the officers' building, seeming a little dumfounded.

"Okay, Kamenko," said Frank. "Dinnich can sign for Vaida, but where are these girls' parents?"

Hradich stared at him like he had two heads. "What you mean?"

"Well, you signed permission for your daughter. And Dinnich will sign for Vaida. But the other girls need permission from their parents for the operation."

Hradich picked up the AK-47 and said, "Parents give girls to me. I give permission." He simply turned and went off after Dinnich and the girls.

Frank saw Richter leaning against the building, now with his arms crossed, looking him over intently.

FIFTEEN

The next day was just like the day they did Zivka. Except they did it five times.

The girls had their tents inserted the night before. Each time Frank got his first glimpse, he saw that the willow had expanded nicely. Each time he cleaned out the womb, he looked at the glass suction bottle in the corner, swirling and splashing red.

By the time he got to the fourth girl, he thought he was getting a little immune to the whole process. *What am I doing here? Why is this so easy?*

Later in the day, when he said to Gwen, "Glad I carved all those extra tents?" she didn't say a thing.

He thought about her lack of response as he was lying alone in bed that night, wondering if he had upset her. Wondering if there was something about the whole process that only a woman could understand. Certain he was right about that.

He had an empty feeling in the pit of his stomach and wanted her beside him. Her warmth, her soothing touch. Even her gibes. But she was in the recovery room, sleeping with the girls.

In the morning, Gwen was already up and getting the girls ready for breakfast when he got to the recovery room.

They'd all had a good night. No ill effects.

Gwen was smiling when she said, "All right girls, let's go get some food."

They marched out of recovery and across the square. Five sombre little Yugoslavian grandmas in black, followed by Gwen and Frank.

He touched her shoulder.

She stopped momentarily, smiled broadly and said, "You done good, Doctor."

That was all he needed.

In the canteen, Frank said, "What have you got for us, Dayna?"

"Well, my golly," the cook said, a broad smile across her cherubic, black face. "Step right up, little ladies. I got scrambled eggs, and lots of 'em. Enough for seconds. And toast. And milk." She chortled as she served them.

He wondered for a moment where Jennifer was, but realized she had probably gone to the village to get supplies. The way she always did. He dismissed the thought.

Frank was watching them eat, surprised at their enthusiasm for ketchup on their eggs and the thick jam on their toast.

Some time into second helpings, one of the girls was looking at him, chewing a mouthful. Then she actually smiled at him. It wasn't just a smile, more like a window into a happy soul through twinkling brown eyes.

"Zara!" Dinnich was just entering the canteen, scowling at her.

She averted her gaze immediately and became expressionless.

Frank looked over at him, hoping Dinnich didn't register his contempt.

Gwen squeezed his knee under the table.

Later, Hradich was standing behind the pickup truck, his gun over his shoulder on a sling.

"Okay," he said as the girls filed by. "Say thank you to doctor and nurse."

Five little thank-you's as they walked by.

The girl who had smiled at him didn't look up.

Frank wondered what they had been told by their elders. What was going on in their heads? How did they feel about the process? Did they even have a choice?

They got in the back of the pickup to sit on a wooden bench, and Dinnich closed the tailgate.

Hradich said, "Come back Thursday." He pronounced it *Thoorsday.* "Five more girls."

"We'll see you then," said Frank.

When Dinnich had said his thanks, Hradich took Frank's hand in both of his and said, "Thank you, doctor, so much. You big friend." And gave him a hug.

For a moment, Frank believed it.

The truck pulled away, and one smiling pair of eyes secretly glanced at him.

***

Thursday came. So did Hradich and Dinnich with five more girls. Just like the Monday group, the girls rode in the back of the pickup. Just like them, the girls were very sombre, none of them making eye contact. Walking in behind Gwen, all in a row. An obedient group of girls.

Behaving for their elders.

Until one of them saw something on the other side of the square. She looked down suddenly. Hiding her face—but following the other girls with quick steps.

Frank looked over to see the back of Father John with his face down, hurrying to the main door.

He looked to the girl and saw her right behind Gwen, obviously reluctant to look back.

He wanted to know more, but decided to get on to the next thing. Even though it left him with an uneasy feeling.

Hradich signed for all of the girls again, and Frank thought he'd have to work out a more appropriate consent procedure. The question was how?

The two Bosnian Serbs left the girls behind, without any apparent concern, for the medics to work their magic. Erase the crimes that had been committed in this war.

It was the same drill all over again. Examine the girls. Insert the tents. Have them sleep one night. Give them the Versed and Ketamine. Curette and suction the womb.

Every time, Frank saw the hissing suction container on the wall, swirling and bubbling with the remnants of lost life. But somehow, every time, it was getting just so much easier for him.

***

Gwen was carrying the bucket out after the abortions.

Frank and the duty sergeant had dug a long pit to dump the remains into at the end of every day's work. The remains would go in and some of the dirt would be placed over the new pour, one after another in a row. This was on the edge of the hill, past the north side of the main building.

Gwen was just getting to the corner of the building when a voice alarmed her. She pressed her back into the building and peered carefully around the corner.

Father John was standing over the side of the pit, facing away from her, with his vestments on.

She didn't know he had any vestments—But why shouldn't he?

Straining to hear, she pushed back into the stone wall of the building, out of sight. She clutched the bucket close in her arms so that it wouldn't make any noise against the wall, the mass of red tissue and fluid open for her to see, and smell.

It seemed Father was sobbing. Then she barely made out the words that followed.

"By permission of Pope Benedict XV, I pray for you," some sniffles, "and commend you to the mercy of God." Sobbing. Then he regained control. "Lord God, I call upon you; I will deliver to you these children, who are not sinners, although their parents and protectors are, that you may glorify them with your mercy. Amen."

Gwen wasn't going over there. She imagined what it might do to him. Besides, he needed to own *his* secret.

Father John started The Lord's Prayer.

Gwen stole back to the clinic and left the bucket on the floor, in a corner by the autoclave.

She'd tell Frank what she saw.

***

They kept the girls overnight, but both Frank and Gwen were beginning to wonder if that was really necessary. Their confidence in the procedure was growing. Besides, that was how it was done back home. In. Out. Gone. Only here, it might not be that easy for a sick girl with some complication to come back.

Before going to bed Friday night, Frank decided to start a journal about the abortions they had done. He entered the condition of each girl and their emotional state, starting with Zivka. He didn't tell Gwen about it.

Saturday at noon, Hradich and Dinnich returned to collect the girls.

Frank said, "Kamenko. What if I give you the papers to have the parents sign?"

"Why?" He seemed puzzled. "I sign. I responsible."

Frank knew he wouldn't have any chance of knowing who had really signed them any way. Wartime rules would probably protect them legally, in a pinch.

The girls were in back of the truck when Hradich reached into a backpack and pulled out another bottle of slivovitz.

"Kamenko. No."

Hradich thrust it firmly into Frank's hand, patted his shoulder and said, "You *big* friend."

Frank held the bottle behind his back as the truck drove off. No smiling eyes this time.

He turned to Gwen and said, "How come all the names around here end in *ich?*"

SIXTEEN

"Major. Colonel Richter wants to see you as soon as possible." The soldier in the blue helmet stared down at him.

Frank looked up from his breakfast, "I keep telling you, I'm not a major any more."

"Sir, it's that Air Force thing..."

"Never fucking mind."

"Sir, that's not Air Force either. But sir, really. He wants to see you."

"When?"

"Ten minutes ago."

Frank rapped on Richter's door.

"Come in."

Richter got up, motioned broadly, and said, "Ah. Major Lambert. Do come in." He motioned to the man in the green leather chair. "Major, may I introduce you to Drago Babic."

Frank extended his hand, but the man did not, clutching his beret nervously.

"Please sit down," said Richter.

Frank sat in the other leather chair, throwing curious glances at Drago Babic.

"Major..." Richter sat back into his creaky chair. "Mr. Babic has told me the most interesting story." He nodded knowingly at Frank. "Would you care to hear his story?"

"Of course, I would," said Frank as he looked at Babic and smiled.

"Eh ... eh..." Babic seemed unable to find words.

Richter, waiting and growing impatient, said, "Perhaps I can sum it up for you." He was waiting for a response, but getting none, he said, "Maybe—I—tell your story.

Babic looked at Richter like he was a little confused, and said, "Ya."

Richter turned to Frank. "Mr. Babic comes from a village twenty kilometres north of here. Krovenz. So, he is technically out of our Liaison's territory." Frank looked askance. "Would you be surprised if I told you, Major Lambert, that he has a group of young girls, eh, women, with a problem?" Richter leaned forward, staring seriously at Frank. More like he had contempt for him.

Frank turned to Babic and said, "Really?" trying to put on his compassionate face.

Babic, clutched his beret with tears welling up in his eyes. He looked at Frank and said, "Ya." He wiped his eyes. His lips quivered when he said, "They rape."

Richter made a broad, throw-away gesture with his right hand and settled back in his creaky chair.

"I see," said Frank. He put his hand over onto Babic's.

The man seemed to penetrate Frank with his stare. "I hear you fix. You fix very good."

"Ah," said Richter. "Good news travels fast." He turned to Frank, his eyebrows arched. "You see, Major?"

"I see." Frank looked back at Babic and said, "How many?"

He took his time, staring intently at Frank, maybe to determine if he had transgressed. Then Babic said, "Twenty-one."

"Tell me," said Frank, "who raped these girls?"

"Men from other village."

"Do you know these men?"

"No."

"What happens to your boys?"

"Boys?" Babic paused. "They go for work."

"Do they come home?"

"Not yet."

"Very well," said Frank. "How can we contact you?"

Babic reached into his tunic, pulled out a piece of paper and handed it to Frank.

"The colonel and I will think this over," said Frank. "If we can, we'll start with five girls next Thursday. But we will call you with instructions."

"Thank you," Babic said to Richter. "Thank you, Major Doctor."

Richter said, "It's good. You can go."

Babic let himself out.

"Well, that was refreshing," said Frank. "No AK-47."

Richter looked at Frank. "Why Thursday and not Wednesday?"

"I don't want him bumping into Hradich around here. Each of them with five girls." Frank levelled his gaze at Richter. "And he *is* intruding in Hradich's territory. Besides, he's a Muslim."

"I know," said Richter.

SEVENTEEN

Hradich's group had arrived on time. The girls got their cervical tents that evening and their procedures the next day.

It was with the fourth one, while staring at the bottle on the wall, when Frank knew something had gone wrong. Had he pushed too hard with the curette? He was certain he had perforated her uterus—just by the feel.

Why was he always staring at the bottle? Why did it hold him that way?

He told Gwen.

"So what do we do?" she said.

"How's our antibiotic supply?"

"Not good, but we have some Cipro and Flagyl."

"That'll do," said Frank. "We'll get it set up as soon as we finish the next one."

Once they had the last procedure done, Frank being very ginger with the curette, they set up the antibiotic IV on the fourth girl.

Frank told the duty officer to notify Hradich that the girls would be one day late. "Supplies," he had told him, chastising himself for lying. But then would Hradich even care?

"Tell Babic not to come until Friday," he said.

Not like we need weekends off.

He reminded himself to enter her complications into his journal.

Tajana, the girl with the perforation, was okay on Thursday morning. Her belly was soft. She ate well. Frank was happy letting her go with medication to take by mouth.

Hradich arrived at noon and said, "What is problem?"

"I needed to give Tajana extra medicine." He gave a packet to Hradich and said, "This one, the white one, she takes two times every day for seven days. This capsule she takes four times a day for seven days."

Hradich seemed to look through him. "You good friend."

He left with the girls in the back of the truck.

***

Thursday night, Frank was lying in bed with his leg over Gwen's torso. He had scratched her back and was rubbing her abdomen, which she liked, when she flinched.

"Ow!"

"What's the matter?"

"I've got this sore spot on my ankle." She looked at him. "My left ankle. Think I scraped it on a gurney.

"Sorry."

"Don't be. You didn't know."

They rolled left, Frank cradling her, and they were soon asleep.

***

Drago Babic showed up on time, Friday afternoon, driving a van. There was another man with him.

He opened the side door of the van, letting out the five girls. Three wore black dresses, but one girl's was dark green and the others' dark blue. All full length, and they all had scarves on their heads, either black or white. They actually had slight smiles, and four of them said, "Hallo." The one in blue went over to Babic and put her arm around him.

"She's yours?" said Frank.

"Ya." He put his arm on her shoulder, and said, "Is Iman."

She broke into a broad smile, her brown eyes holding Frank's, as she said, "Hallo," almost cheerfully.

"Hello, Iman," said Frank. "I'm glad you've come to see us. We are going to help you." *Don't need to tell her not to be afraid.*

She looked up at her father with an adoring smile that showed teeth. She squeezed his waist and leaned on his shoulder.

***

Frank said to Gwen, "What a change!"

That afternoon they had given the injections of Gravol, examined the girls and placed the willow tents in all five. They were in the canteen eating. The light was subdued.

"Um-hmm," she said. "Not like the others."

"No AK-47s." He looked at her. "And it's like they really appreciate what we're doing."

"Don't get too excited." She squeezed his wrist between bites. "Let's get these girls done. See what happens. Then see how the next batch goes." She bobbed her head from side to side. "Before we count our chickens."

"Maybe you're right." Frank thought for a moment, and said, "Do you remember last Thursday's group?"

"Yeah. Why?"

"The last one in behind you—She was shorter than the others."

"What about her?" Gwen's eyes narrowed.

"Did she seem especially nervous to you?"

"She's one of Hradich's. They're all pretty up tight, don't you think?" She waited a second. "Why?"

Frank spoke slowly. "She got out of the truck and followed behind you. So you didn't catch this. When she saw Father John, she became anxious. I mean real anxious. Kept her head down, like she was panicked."

"So?"

"Father John did the same but headed off in the other direction." He leaned back and turned his palms up, as if to ask *why*.

"You tell Richter?"

Frank shook his head.

Gwen looked at him. "It was after that batch of girls that I saw him out back, praying."

"You see him there again?"

"No."

EIGHTEEN

Frank and Gwen began early in the morning. The routine was the same as for Hradich's girls. They'd get the Ketamine anaesthetic and some Versed IV. Then they'd spread their legs. He would insert the speculum and pull out the wood tent. Some of the girls weren't even fully asleep. That was the beauty of the drug. They didn't require respirators. Which made Ketamine the number-one battlefield anaesthetic in the world. Then the small dose of Versed kept them from remembering anything.

One after another, Frank curetted the inside of their wombs and then suctioned them out. Every time he marvelled at the glass suction bottle in the corner of the room, reddening.

It occurred to him that he was systematically taking more and more lives. The lives of the unborn. And he knew that it wasn't bothering him—not even a pang of guilt. He was giving the girls and their families back their lives.

He was sure Gwen felt the same, but they hadn't really talked about it.

Later that evening, he said to her, "I've been thinking about this. Like we discussed the other day. We don't really need to keep the girls overnight afterward. Now that we're used to the process." He paused. "I mean, unless something goes wrong. Then we'd keep the girl around." He looked at her. She seemed puzzled. "That's how they do it in the States."

"But Frank. I've been thinking about it too. This isn't the States. What if something goes wrong?"

"Well, I'll know if I perforate one. We'll keep her. They all have instructions. They know they'll bleed for a week. If they get a fever, they know to come back."

She looked at him.

He said, "Not really that much to it."

Gwen said, "It might not be that easy for them to get back here."

"I feel better that way about this bunch."

"Let me think about it."

***

Babic showed up on time to pick up his girls and drop off five others.

He came to Frank, making a bit of a show in front of the girls, and said, "Thank you, Major Doctor."

"You're welcome," said Frank.

"You are big help." He turned to the girls and said, "Say thank you to doctor."

A chorus of "Thank you's".

Babic said, "I see with my eyes, you take good care of girls. I thank you. Other families thank you. We pay somehow. Favour. Anything."

"It's not necessary. We're here to help."

Frank saw Colonel Richter across the square, watching. He wondered what he must be thinking,

He turned back as Babic, and the other man drove away with the girls.

The five new ones were being herded to their quarters by another nurse. There was one who was a bit different. She was taller and quite striking. She wore a deep red kerchief.

Frank turned to Gwen and said, "Here we go again."

"There's just one problem," said Gwen. "I've done an inventory. We've got enough drugs and supplies for a few more groups."

"So?"

"We're going to run out of willow tents. By the end of the week at this rate."

"Shit! And you thought I carved too many."

"Well, we didn't know *this* was going to happen."

"Right." He thought a moment. "I'll get Hradich to drop off another bough."

"What will you tell him? We need them for other girls. Ones he hasn't brought in?"

It came to him right away. "I'll tell him I want to carve some more, just in case."

NINETEEN

The five girls got done the usual way. There were no problems. They were bedded down for the night with one of the duty nurses, which left Frank and Gwen free to spend some time in the canteen.

After dinner, Gwen said, "You know what I'd like?"

"What?"

"I'd like a nice glass of wine. White wine. I almost can't remember the last time."

"Well, we're shit out of luck on that front. But we do have some of Hradich's slivovitz."

"That crap is rocket fuel. Made to get you drunk."

"I could use you a little drunk."

"Hm." She smiled at him coyly.

"Then let's go to my room."

They left the canteen and crossed the darkened square, hand in hand.

"How does that song go?" said Frank. "I should have mixed some water with the wine."

Back in his room, Frank closed the shutters and lowered the light to one small bulb. He pulled his clothes off before getting the bottle from the cupboard. He poured some liquor into two glasses as he watched Gwen undress. Then he added some water and sat down at the table.

She came to him. As she stood in front of him, he kissed her right in her shaved pubic hair and then both her nipples.

Gwen bent down, kissing him full in the mouth. She pulled Frank up, holding him tight with her left arm and massaging him into a full erection. She backed off a little and took a mouthful of her drink.

Frank did the same and then pulled her over to the bed. They got in and Gwen put her leg over Frank's thigh. He let his hand down between her legs and rubbed her a moment, feeling she was smooth and wet. He rolled onto her, ready to enter. He moved his foot over her left ankle.

"Ah!" she cried and pulled her leg away.

"What's the matter?"

"Oh God." She bent down and rubbed her ankle. "Oh, that hurts."

"What?"

"It's that damn spot I scraped on the gurney in the operating room."

"Let me take a look."

"There's nothing to see. I've been rubbing it with alcohol every day, and there's nothing to see, I tell you. It just hurts so much when I bump it."

"All right then. But I'm looking at it tomorrow."

She leaned forward and kissed him.

"Here, roll on your left and get your leg comfortable."

He tucked in behind her and held her around the waist.

They were soon asleep.

***

First thing in the morning, Frank inspected her ankle. There was nothing to see, but she was very tender on the bone above the inside knuckle of her left ankle.

Frank said, "I don't like that."

"What do you think it is?"

"Maybe just a bruise to the bony lining. At least, that's what I'm hoping."

He looked up at her. They were both still completely naked.

"Anyway, we need to get organized before Babic gets here."

They saw the girls just after they got dressed and took them over to the canteen, where Dayna had made another fantastic breakfast.

"Come on in," she said in her southern drawl. "There's enough for everybody to have seconds. And I've got lots of ketchup."

"You learn fast, girl," said Frank.

"Hey. I know howta keep ma people happy. Heh, heh, heh."

They were finished by ten, just in time for Jennifer to show up, unloading the food supplies out of the transport.

Frank noticed that Dayna ignored her, as if on purpose. Once again, he didn't get it.

Then Babic pulled up in his van, but the man with him was different. He was younger than the others. Not clean-shaven. He looked like he was a hard worker. And of all things, he wore a plaid jacket.

They got out of the van, and Babic said, "I see everything good."

"Yeah, it's all good," said Frank. "You remember the instructions— what you have to watch for?"

"For sure, I remember."

The girls got into the van, saying their "Thank you's". All so appreciative. The man in the plaid jacket seemed especially interested in the girl with the deep red kerchief.

Frank remembered that her name was Mia. And he thought the father's name was Moustaffa. When they were all in the van, Babic came over to Frank and spoke softly. "Maybe I ask you something?"

"Sure." Frank thought he knew what it was going to be.

"I have more girls." He cast his eyes to the ground momentarily, before looking up.

Bingo. Frank said, "How many?"

"Fifteen for sure. Maybe twenty." He looked at Frank, maybe a bit desperate.

"I'll see what I can do." He nodded. "I think I need supplies."

Babic cocked his head, like he didn't understand.

"I need more medicine. . ."

TWENTY

Colonel Richter sat there behind his desk, looking at him with a pained expression that could mean only one thing.

Frank said, "You called for me?"

"Um…" Richter shifted in his seat, not saying anything for a moment. And then, "You are short on supplies." He paused, "But you need to speak to Hradich. Why now? Why not the next time he drops some girls off?"

"Because at this rate we won't be doing any more girls." Frank sat down in one of the green leather chairs.

Richter said, "Is there something wrong with that?"

"Well, we're not finished."

"You mean…?"

"Yes. Babic has committed to fifteen more girls, and I'm sure Hradich will have more."

Richter leaned back in his chair, looking very displeased.

"So, when Hradich arrives, we can't tell him we're doing girls he hasn't brought here. Do you understand, Kurt?"

"Of course I understand." Richter sat up, looking around, distracted. "But what do you need from Hradich?"

"I thought you knew. I need another dry willow bough, so I can carve some more tents."

"Because?" He gestured wide with an open palm.

"We're running out. We've done thirty-five girls."

"You've *done?*" said Richter. "You mean you've aborted." He stared at Frank. "Why can't you doctors ever say what it is you've done? Instead you say, *we've done.*"

"You're right Kurt, I mean colonel."

Richter was nodding. "And tents. Tents are where soldiers sleep, in the field." He waited a moment. "Whoever called a piece of dry wood, one you jam up a woman's vagina to expedite an abortion, a tent?"

"I think it was the British that started it, in the sixties."

"Ah, the British." He waved his finger at Frank. "That makes sense too."

Both men sat in silence for some time. The tension was palpable.

Finally, Frank said, "I need to work out another plan."

"Like?"

"I'm not sure. I need to think this over. Maybe discuss it with someone." Frank thought for a moment. "I'm going to call an old friend in Paris. A gynaecologist."

Richter's mouth gaped open. He waved his finger *no*, at Frank. "You're not bringing a gynaecologist here from Paris."

"Oh no. Of course not. I just need to discuss my options. I'll try to call him today. Figure something out."

"Okay, I'll arrange for a call."

"One more thing." He saw the expression on Richter's face and thought, *Strange Prussian charm.* "Do you think I can get out to Europe for a couple of days? To France?"

"France I cannot do. However, I could get you to Ramstein on the transport from Sarajevo. Assuming the road is open and the supply truck comes. Goes every Tuesday and Thursday."

"That would work perfectly. Tuesday then."

"Very well. That means no abortions next week."

"Right. Besides which, I need that willow bough from Hradich."

"I'll let him know."

"My cell has no service again."

"The sergeant will help you."

"Thank you, Colonel."

"It is always a pleasure assisting you, Major." Richter sarcastic, and alluding to his old rank. "Goodbye, Frank."

They stood up and shook hands.

"Goodbye, Kurt."

On his way out, Frank stopped at the duty sergeant's desk.

"I need to speak to a Claude Savigny, in Paris. I have permission from Colonel Richter."

"Sir, do you have any idea how many Claude Savignys there must be in and around Paris?"

"This one's a gynaecologist."

"Oh well…" He shrugged.

Frank cocked his head and regarded him with a look of displeasure.

The duty sergeant became serious. "That should narrow it down." He busied himself with the satellite phone.

Frank barely had time to pace twice around the office.

"Here it is, sir." He handed him the phone. "Just push *call* to connect."

Frank pushed the red button and heard the system clicking to make the call. Then the soft beep-beep of the phone ringing.

A soothing female voice answered, "*Ici Bureau de Dr. Claude Savigny. Bonjour.*"

He said, "Hello. This is Dr. Frank Lambert. I am an old friend of Dr. Savigny, and I'm trying to get in touch with him."

"*Oui.* He is 'ere. I will connect you."

When the gravelly voice came on, Frank felt a rush of warmth come over him.

"Frank. Frank Lambert. Is it really you?"

"Yes, Claude. *Comment ça va?*"

"I am doing well. But you sound like you are on another planet."

"I am in Yugoslavia. Working a relief mission. I'm on a satellite phone."

"Of course, you are."

"Claude, I have a problem that I need to discuss with you. And I may need your help."

Frank felt another rush when Claude said, "Tell me all about it."

***

Upstairs, Richter was having some cognac. He had turned the lights down to one dim bulb after Frank had left. He was leaning back in his chair with his feet up on his desk and the glass in his right hand.

The light was subdued.

Frank Lambert was the topic of his ruminations.

Frank had arrived with a peerless recommendation from his NGO. The surgeon cared for his patients—to a fault.

But the Bundeswehr Military Police dossier labeled (Major) Frank Lambert—USA, (Retired), was a different matter.

Richter had read it.

The dossier described a surgeon who was a workaholic alcoholic. Attending patients around the clock only to be dredged up later, from some den of iniquity by the MPs. As much an asset to his patients as he was a danger to his comrades.

For Richter the issue was that he didn't have any such luxury. He had to tow the line. Strictly. And that was his reputation—peerless adherence and obedience to his superiors.

Richter wondered about the man seven years his junior. The one who had followed his father's footsteps to become a tactical pilot. Then went to medical school and became a surgeon instead. Had Flight Surgeon status and could probably still fly after a short break-in. And then retired from the air force. Divorced. Like he had yielded to every single one of his life's desires. He had walked every road, rounded every corner, explored every field. Only to end up in Rwanda, and now here, sleeping with the beautiful black nurse and doing abortions.

Because he thinks it's right?

Richter also came from a military family, but he had never had so many degrees of freedom. He was devoted to his assignments and his superiors—to a fault. Except one. He had never wanted more than that. Never wanted to become a doctor. Never thought of being a surgeon. Never thought his soul could harbor an ounce of jealousy. Until now.

Colonel Kurt Richter of the Bundeswehr was decorated and un-blemished.

He was also a realist and took care of himself.

TWENTY-ONE

Hradich showed up Saturday morning with the new willow bough and a large measure of curiosity. They met outside Frank's quarters.

"Why you need more wood?"

"Because I used the other one up."

"But it was big willow."

"Kamenko, I've never done this before. So I had to practice carving, and some wood was wasted. I couldn't use it." He waited for some kind of a response. "Besides, you're going to bring me more girls. Aren't you?"

"Maybe yes, more girls."

"Of course you are. So, I'm going to be ready for them. Besides." He was measuring whether he should let it slip, or not. "Maybe there are other girls. Ones you don't bring to me? They will need help too."

Frank thought he saw a flicker of Hradich's eyelids. A momentary narrowing triggered by disdain?

"And you are the UN Liaison. The UN is here to help everybody. Am I right?"

"Ya sure. UN help everybody."

It was the way he had said it. *Ya sure...* An unexpected decrescendo. For Frank it was more of a tone he associated with loss. So what could Hradich think he was losing? Control? Certainly not. Trust. Unlikely. His favourite willow bough?

Frank said, "So what happens if there are girls from villages, far away, that need my help? Girls that you don't know about. Do I say no?"

It took him a moment, like *he* was putting the genie back in the lamp. Hradich said, "Maybe you help."

***

They were lying in bed, Gwen on her back, Frank with his leg over her thigh, massaging her abdomen through and through. He thought of something he wanted to say and hesitated.

Gwen sensed his slowing and said, "Don't stop. It really feels good. And rub real slow."

Frank had already told her about his talk with Claude Savigny. Claude was going to give him a large supply of morning-after pills. They were going to meet. He was leaving on Monday for Sarajevo to catch the Canadian transport to Ramstein Air Force Base, Germany on Tuesday, returning Thursday night. There would be no abortions all next week.

"So," Gwen said, "exactly how are we going to get this stuff out there? It's not like we're a walk-in clinic."

"We'll just have to get the word out that if it's a fresh rape, they have two days to get the medicine. The rest we'll have to do the way we have been. With D&Cs."

"And you think that will work?"

"Look. At some point these people have to do their part. They need to participate in the process. Otherwise we won't be able to keep up. And we're *it*, baby."

"And how many pills is he giving you?"

"Four thousand. That's enough to do one thousand girls."

"Jesus Christ!" She thought a moment. "How does he get his hands on that much?"

90

"Hey. He's Claude from Boston. The guru of gynaecology in Paris. Drug companies would line up to do him a favor—a big favor. And he's persuasive."

"He's your buddy. How come you're so different?"

"Opposites, I guess. So this weekend, I carve tents. Hradich brought me a new bough. You sterilize them while I'm away. Then we get going."

"Okay."

"What I didn't tell you, was about Hradich."

"Like?"

"Well, he was a little bit off."

"How?"

"When I told him about needing more tents and the fact that we might be doing more girls that he didn't bring here, he was well, just off. Like he had lost control or something." Frank thought a moment. "Do you remember when he first talked to us, about his daughter?"

"Yes."

"I got the idea that he came to us and got exactly what he wanted."

"Of course, he did."

"Yeah, but I remember looking at him, and thinking that *he* had just taken charge or something. Anyway, it was a little weird. It just took me back to that moment."

Gwen said, "Well, this is the Balkans. And these people are different."

Frank said, "I know, it's probably just a cultural thing, but it bothers me."

"Hey, the UN says he's clean."

"The UN says a lot of things. And don't forget these people started World War One with a single shot to a prince named Freddie. They've been writing history here for a long time."

"Stop obsessing about Hradich and concentrate on me."

TWENTY-TWO

She had made her plans carefully. She knew the exact time at which the duty officer left his post. The relief station shut down every night. There was no reason to keep it open. All the important communication was by satellite phone, which the duty officer took to bed with him. The colonel had one too. If there was a reason to open up, they could be reached.

That was her main risk. They might receive an urgent patient at night. But that had only happened once. The girls came and went during the day. Right now there weren't any patients here at all. And the surgeon had left that evening for Sarajevo, to fly to Germany for some reason.

The timing couldn't have been better.

She knew that earlier in the day, *he* had checked the lock on the back door of the main building. The door no-one ever used or looked at because it was to be permanently locked.

She had her backpack with her, as she carefully walked between the buildings. She had rehearsed the route a number of times, making certain there were no surprises. Like rocks to trip on. Or twigs to crack.

She quickly stole across the central square to the far side of the main building, where she couldn't be seen. There wasn't even a moon.

How perfect is that?

She got out her penlight and quickly got to the door.

With her gloved hand she turned the old knob and pushed gently. The door wouldn't yield.

For a second, she felt a sense of panic and her heart sped up.

But he had partially jimmied the lock open that very day. She wasn't going to get any second chances. And she wasn't going to trust *him*. It was tonight or never.

She leaned harder into the door. Something inside went clunk and the door moved inward, slightly.

She held perfectly still, trying to determine if anybody had heard; that there might be someone coming. She turned her light off.

She spent a few long minutes, straining to hear the sound of a door, or footsteps on the gravelly soil. Even though she was on the far side of the building, she ought to be able to hear something.

No dangerous sounds revealed themselves.

She turned the penlight back on and entered the storage room. From there it was into the main office, past the gun locker, over to the clinic door. A quick look at the tarpaulined windows. No sign of a light approaching.

She thanked her combat training.

Once inside the clinic, her job was easy.

She found the drug locker. Without the key—Gwen the bitch had that—she would improvise.

The yellow-handled screwdriver came out of her pocket, and went to work. She was in almost immediately.

Her employers had told her what to look for. The metal bins yielded a treasure-trove. Everything she wanted. Things that ended in "contin". Fentanyl. Percocet. Morphine. And antibiotics. Cipro. Clinda—she forgot the ending—but got the drug. Flagyl, Metronidazole and Penicillins—leave behind. No real street value.

She was stuffing her backpack. It was full to overflowing.

Then she thought she heard something. Unsure of what it was, she went to the window and peeled the tarpaulin back, gingerly. Getting a look didn't help. Nothing seemed to be wrong. The buildings opposite were dark.

Need to get out of here.

She went to the duty office and closed the clinic door. Back to the storage room. She loosened the lock on the door. Opened and shut it three times, ever so gently, to make sure it worked. Then, let herself out.

She felt better outside. Like she could breathe again. She shouldered the sack and carefully retraced her steps on the far side of the building.

Coming around the far corner by the door, she saw it, and immediately pulled back.

There was a red ember glowing in front of one of the buildings.

Her heart raced. She breathed faster, but immediately calmed herself down.

Has to be Mike. The second duty officer. He was always complaining he couldn't sleep. Up at night, smoking.

Does this shit have to happen now?

She would just have to wait him out. Hopefully, she wouldn't have to subdue him.

That wouldn't go well.

Hard to argue your way out of that one. Especially if they discovered the clinic stores were missing.

And I can't get in to put them back.

She leaned against the wall, quietly. Carefully. So as not to make a sound.

She would just have to wait him out. She peered around the edge of the building and wished she had her camouflage on her face.

The fucker's lighting another cigarette!

She leaned back against the building and took a few deep breaths as she took her gloves off.

For a second she wished she wasn't there. Wished she was back home.

But that was not the reality of the situation. She had put herself here. And she needed the money.

If all went well, she would get back to her room and put the pack below the removable panel in the floor she had found. Then the next day, she would go to town, as she always did. She would get her money. *But not if Mike's going to keep smoking.*

She timed herself by counting, the way she had been trained. Six minutes. He was a hurried smoker.

She peered around the corner, just in time to see the glowing butt fly into the square. She heard the door close softly.

She'd wait another five minutes. Just to be sure. Give him time to fall back asleep.

As she counted, she looked around. Some stars visible through partial overcast. The dark outlines of the neighboring hills that could hide a thousand eyes. But she was in the shadows too. Invisible. What would have been seen if anybody was watching, was Mike's cigarette. Probably long enough for a sniper to target him. But, up until this point, nobody had bothered them here.

Hope that continues.

Finally, she retraced her steps. Between the buildings. Across the square. Back to her quarters.

She'd hardly made a sound.

Letting herself in, the door co-operated.

Luckily, they all shared rooms with only one other.

Carefully, across the floor and into her room.

Silently, stash the pack.

Undress and into bed.

She thought a moment before falling asleep. With Frank Lambert gone for a few days, nobody would even notice the missing drugs, because no medical work would be done.

Perfect.

TWENTY-THREE

The Hercules yawed on approach then touched the landing strip with a thump—none of the rattling and shaking of a commercial airliner. The groan of reverse thrust. About a mile down the runway they sped past concrete bunkers like large upside-down pound cakes hiding the odd F-15. They passed a wing of F-16s going up the taxiway.

The plane finally came to rest near a set of small green buildings, and, when Frank disembarked down the stairway he was met by an officer who snapped to attention and saluted. Frank didn't.

"Welcome to Ramstein, sir!"

"Right."

"Your orders?"

Frank looked at him. Slim. Polished. Eager. Twenty-one, if he was a day. Frank waited, and said, "Really?"

"Report to the officer's mess." There was less urgency in the voice. "You've been assigned a room. Report to General Carter at your earliest convenience, sir."

"Understood. Would you tell the general that I'd like to shower, and I'll see him right after, if that's okay."

"At your convenience."

"Thanks," said Frank as they strode out from under the cargo plane, "and would you inform the general that I don't intend to stay long. I plan to rent a car and get going before noon." He handed the officer his bag and looked up to the right. Nearby, stood a giant plane with its body broken open on a hinge—a plane that looked like it could swallow a 747. He felt a shiver as he turned away from the transport.

An hour later, he was in the general's office.

General Carter, a big, burly man, extended his hand as he came over. "Good to see you, Frank." He pumped Frank's hand with both of his. "Travel arrangements good?"

"Yes. Very good, thanks."

"Not at all." The general waved as he sat down behind his desk. "Not the easiest thing getting out of Yugoslavia these days. Good thing NATO still controls the airport in Sarajevo. They don't control much else." He shook his head. "And I figured if you're going… where in France?"

"Beaune."

"Beaune! Going to drink a little wine?" He chortled and paused. "Not a bad idea after where you've been. Anyway," he shook his head slightly, "Ramstein is as good as any place to start."

"I really appreciate your help, Vern," said Frank as he sat on a brown leather couch in the darkly panelled office.

The big man rolled up his sleeves, leaned forward and cocked his head. He waited a moment, looking at Frank so as to absorb him. "What are you really up to?"

Vern Carter was like an uncle. Frank didn't mind the questions. "I'm meeting a friend from Paris to get some help for the relief effort."

"Right. And you're with who?"

Frank said, I'm with Forward Doctors International. It's a new NGO."

"Only now you're at an advance relief station, in uncontrolled territory, trying to help the Bosnians."

"Well, the area isn't held by NATO, and we're doing some good. There's a genocide going on, you know. Just nobody's noticed."

"So I've heard. Now you know what Congress thinks about the UN. They're slow. Witless. And what's worse, spineless. That's why we're getting out of there. It would be like *hurry up and wait*, while the world takes shots at us. No point!" He seemed curious about what Frank would say.

"You're right about that."

Carter's gaze pierced Frank. "And there you are again, stuck in the thick of things."

"The end justifies the means."

A smile of understanding crept over the general's face. "You know, I still consider you Air Force. You can still pull rank around here." He seemed to wait for Frank's response. Nothing. "Ever consider coming back?" Frank shook his head. "What about Liz and the kids?"

"Back in the States. I see them when I work in Boston. Things haven't changed…" He stared at the floor. Feeling a pang of shame in front of Vern.

General Carter came over and put his arm on Frank's shoulder. "I'm sorry, Frank. I don't mean to make you feel bad—just, you're like *my* son, and *I* don't have any. Your father was the best friend I ever had." His sincerity radiated. "And he was one of the best goddamned pilots in the air force. He could fly circles around anything. I don't have to tell you that. What happened was tragic. I still feel responsible. What can I say? What can I do?" The two men embraced for a long moment and then pulled apart. "I'll do whatever I can for you."

"Actually," Frank thought the time was coming, "I think I need to get moving if I'm going to make Beaune by tonight. I need to rent a car."

"You'll use my car!"

"I have money, Vern."

"Nonsense," the general protested, raising a hand. "I insist. When are you coming back?"

"Tomorrow. I plan to make Thursday's transport to Sarajevo." Frank picked up his bag.

"Here. I'll show you to the car." They walked a corridor to the back of the heavily guarded building. A soldier with a submachine gun snapped to attention and saluted as they stepped out the back door. "That's it." The general pointed like an indulgent father and handed Frank the key.

Frank smiled when he saw the solid black Porsche Turbo. It was one of the older ones. He opened the door to the tan interior and threw his bag in the back. "Thanks." He shook the general's hand.

"Not my first choice in colour, perhaps, but there still are some advantages to the air force." He chortled as he turned to go back.

Two hours down the Autobahn, the sign came up for Mulhouse, a large symbol of a castle with an arrow pointing right and the word Frankreich. He held the right lane, made the sweeping corner, and having cleared the wide bridge over the muddy Rhine, slowed for the border crossing.

The road widened to six lanes, and cars were stopped ahead of him for a distance of about one and a half kilometres to the overhead placards and inspection booths. An officer with an orange cross on his jacket and a submachine gun over his shoulder waved him to the far right. A quarter of a kilometre down, another officer waved him to the right, signalled that he should get onto a seventh lane divided by pilons, and motioned him forward. Frank kept driving to the back of the inspection station, where he was waved through and saluted by two armed guards.

That was easy. He depressed the gas and upshifted as the car howled, popped, and merged into three lanes. The black car with American Forces license plate 001 cleared from view of the inspection station.

Once past Belfort, the A-36 was one of those beautiful sweeping six-lane highways that made memories. It clung to the sides of undulating hills, swept past deep green forests, Alsatian vineyards and fallen castles on hilltops. The dips and curves encouraged throwing the

Porsche some throttle just to feel it tear into a corner; 150, 250 even 280 kilometres per hour came up without fuss. He ended up driving around 160, a real sweet spot that he developed a feeling for. He was glad he had Vern's car. Boy, he was glad!

A moment came when Frank wondered why he didn't do more of this—why he spent his time where he did? The road had captured his soul and he felt entirely at peace with himself.

A while later he was on a particularly beautiful stretch, La Comptoise, where he got a good view of Montmirey-le-Château, one of the greatest and most majestic in France, clinging to a slope to the north. Grey sand stones and ramparts glowed with yellow and ochre highlights in the late afternoon sun against velvet green forests, the darkening umber of plowed fields and the deepening blue of the sky—absolutely storybook.

Soon he did the switch onto the A-6 south and a few kilometres later the right turn into Beaune just before night-fall. He drove through the third medieval rock wall into the town centre and parked just across from the round tower-like building that was his objective. Frank knew the town well from previous visits—one even with Liz. He was an hour early. He was happy with the car, with its gaping rear air intakes; he rapped the roof with his right hand. *I'll get one some day.*

Frank took a walk around the town centre. Clusters of stone buildings on cobblestone streets were becoming lit by old street lights that looked unchanged since World War II. He went around to the Hospice De Beaune and caught the last remnants of daylight being sliced by rays of tungsten intruders on the ornate, curved tile roof. He found pleasure and solace in the peaceful shadows and comforting, bucolic smells of the quiet wine town.

At seven he went to Le Saint-Vincent, through one of the archways and the heavy ancient wood door, into a rocky vestibule draped in royal blue fabric and lit with candles.

A waiter, in black pants and starched white shirt, said, "*Monsieur?*"

"*Reservation pour Savigny ou Lambert, a Sept heurs.*" He hoped his French was all right.

"*Suivi.*" He led Frank through a rocky arch into a dining room of sandstone walls interspersed with hardwood tables partly covered in white tablecloths and surrounded by green and red striped velvet chairs.

Frank could see a familiar-looking man rise in the far corner, one with dark hair and a heavy black moustache who started toward him with outstretched hands.

"*Allors.*" The waiter stepped aside and pointed.

The two men met and embraced heartily.

"Claude, you look well," said Frank as he ran his fingers over what felt like a cashmere corduroy jacket of mushroom grey. He ran his hands up the back of his friend's head and pulled him close once more, recognizing the familiar smell of his black hair.

"*Et vous, aussi!*"

Frank felt a little sheepish in blue jeans and blue fleece. He pulled off his all-weather jacket. "Did you bring the package?"

"*Merde!*" Claude punched him in the shoulder. "I haven't seen you in five fucking years; I drive hundreds of kilometres from Paris to see my goddamned friend, and the first words out of your mouth are, do you have the package? *Sacrement!*"

"I'm sorry, Claude." He held his hands out wide.

"Sit down. I'm having a martini." They sat. Claude cast his gaze astray. "I have your package."

A waiter appeared. Frank said, "*La même chose.*" The waiter left. "I didn't mean it that way. It's just that, you know, so much hangs in the balance…"

"For you, *mon ami*, there is always something hanging in the balance. You're lucky you have anything left to hang after what happened in

Rwanda. I couldn't believe the story—you walking down the roads looking for survivors, with the killers still wandering the streets."

"Well, they wouldn't be alive for very long after they've been cut in the hot sun."

"So, Frank is going to save them? Where is your perspective—your common sense—your responsibility for yourself, your family, your loved ones?" He settled a bit, but seemed glad he had said this. "You go and do these things at great risk, *mon ami*, but what of you?"

He felt Claude's anger. "I can tell you our camp is secure."

"That is not the point, Frank. Do you remember those nights on Boylston Street? The Exeter? Fridays?"

"Yes."

"Do you remember what we talked about in those days? We were going to finish Harvard and go light the world on fire. You a surgeon. Me a gynaecologist."

"Well, you're lighting the world on fire in Paris, Claude. You're doing all the beautiful people." He paused. "Me? I still have an appointment in Boston."

"When you're there." He pointed accusingly. "When you're not wading in the rotten spoils of some war to save people from themselves. I'm surprised they let you stay."

"Hey, I'm their token volunteer. I'm their man in the trenches. It looks good on them!" Frank's martini came, and he took a long sip. "Haven't had one of these in a long time."

"*Exactement.* Now explain to me how the surgeon is helping the people of Yugoslavia, and how does that fit with what I brought you?"

"Claude, you know there's a genocide going on."

"If you say so!"

"You just can't see it yet. That will come, as it did in Rwanda. In fact, I've only treated one casualty there in months, and he was a soldier." Frank stared at his friend. Claude slouched dispassionately in his chair.

"Then, a few weeks ago, a town elder came to me about his daughter." Claude's attention sharpened. "He told me his daughter had been raped, and could I do an abortion on her?"

Claude sat upright. "*Non!*"

"Yes!" He looked squarely at Claude. "And I did it. That was just the start of my troubles. The floodgates opened. I got more and more girls coming in for abortions—so many I can't keep up."

"Wait a minute, Frank. This doesn't make sense. Religiously, the people of Yugoslavia would be against abortion. But where do all these girls get pregnant? And how do they reach you?"

"The best I can figure out, like all wars, both sides commit atrocities. For the most part, when a village is purged, it means they kill the men and the boys so they can't fight. But they rape the girls. Hundreds, possibly thousands of them."

"Out of lust, or what?"

"Oh, war lust. Lust after the kill. But think of it. Rape is a time-honoured weapon of war!"

Claude looked perplexed.

Frank continued. "Before there was abortion, your daughter would carry and bear the child that is half your enemy into your midst. But the child is only half your kind. How can you kill your daughter's child?" He put his hand over his heart. "So the child grows, and your agony burns."

"I never thought of it that way."

"Works for both sides. It's demoralizing." Frank drained his martini. "As for the religious aspect, it hasn't come up. I figure, any way these people can outwit each other is okay. Besides, they're desperate."

The waiter came and they ordered.

"And now your plan is?" Claude shrugged.

"There's no way that I can keep on working for the girls. The job is just too big and there's no sign of it letting up. We're running out of supplies. Besides, the NCO isn't very understanding. So I needed an alternative. If I have the pills, then I'll get the word out that any raped girl can see me within a day or so and use the pills instead. Simple really. Save a lot of work."

"Innovation. You surprise me!" Claude shook his head slowly and said, "*Mais non.*"

"Claude, in these places you do what you can with what you have. It becomes part of your makeup."

"And sometimes you call on the help of an old friend." Claude smiled as he swirled his glass, watching the lemon twist spin amidst the cubes. He drained it.

Frank knew that Claude would identify with the girls' plight.

The waiter arrived with two glasses and a bottle of Château Meursault. He poured some, placed the glass in front of Claude and waited. Claude motioned for Frank to try the wine.

Frank looked at the deep straw-coloured liquid. The smell was somewhat sweet, but the taste exploded on his tongue like a handful of buttered walnuts. "Wow!"

Claude leaned across the table and raised his glass for the waiter to fill. "And this is the power of France." He stared at Frank. "*Oui?*"

The two men sat silently for a while. Swirling the wine. Sniffing. Warming the glasses in their palms. Sipping. They talked about the wines from the area.

"Always wondered what this would be like," said Frank. "Now I know. Man, it's good! Just that I've never been able to afford any."

"You see. Life will pass you by!"

"You're relentless."

Dinner came. The waiter made a great flourish of serving off a white-draped trolley. Frank had fish and Claude langustines. There was wild rice and slivers of vegetables sauteed in butter and tarragon. The French and their tarragon.

The men ate largely in silence save for some small talk.

Finally, before finishing, Claude said, "I've got the drugs. They're in the car. You will find it easy to use."

"What is it exactly?"

"Levonorgestrel. High-dose. You have it in the States. It's called Plan B or something, *comme ça*. The girl takes it the day after rape. Two tablets and two the next day."

"That's it?"

"*C'est ça*. In a pinch she can wait until day three to start, but it begins to lose its power," he emphasized with raised eyebrows and a wave of his finger.

Frank liked Claude's talk, slipping in and out of the little idioms of French "Of course it does nothing for sexually transmitted disease."

Claude looked dumbfounded with some rice still in his mouth. "Leave the STD clinic for somebody else, will you?" He stifled a cough and quickly quaffed some wine. "*Merde!*"

Finally outside at Claude's BMW, he opened the trunk and got out a wooden box of about ten by twelve inches. He handed it to Frank. "That's four thousand pills. That's enough to treat a thousand girls." He slammed the trunk closed. "That should keep you busy for a while." He turned, looked directly at Frank and said, "If you need any more, you must leave your present hell hole and come here and join me, where I will pour some more French culture down your throat and try to convert you to civilization."

"I promise." He smiled and walked across the square, followed by Claude, who betrayed a slight weave to his walk. He opened the Turbo and stashed the box behind the seat.

"Nice wheels, as you say."

"Belongs to General Carter. He's like an uncle."

"Nice uncle." Claude surveyed the square as he patted his belly and stretched his legs. "We need to find a wine shop before we go to the motel."

Their motel was a U-shaped structure of one storey that surrounded a swimming pool in its centre. The sprawling motel itself was located between two vineyards on the south side of Beaune. In the lobby and restaurant were display cases of wine. Frank checked the labels, some ornate and gilded, some plain. There were wines that he knew nothing about. He'd never even heard of them. But they were sitting there waiting to be plucked. And they were pricey. The winner, was one priced at roughly $2600 a bottle. Frank was glad he could still do the math, although he was beginning to worry about the price of the rooms.

Claude showed up with the keys. "We have a nice suite near the end of this row." On the way out, he said, "I'll drop our stuff at the room. You go to the pool with the wine." He dug a couple of bottles out of the back seat of his car and gave them to Frank. "Here." He fished around in his pants and produced a corkscrew for his friend. "I'll come right back."

Frank held the corkscrew out in front of him. *Standard Frenchman issue.* He wandered across the drive through some shrubbery up to the large pool surrounded by flaming oil lamps in glass cases. He found a couple of lounge chairs with a small table, sat down and proceeded to uncork a bottle. He strained to see the label and held it closer to a lamp, but he still couldn't see the label. He sniffed the bottle and was surprised by something like light cherry fruit and licorice.

He leaned back in the lounger, put his hands behind his head, and let his gaze drift over the stars.

They were very clear. He relaxed. Found Orion. Both Dippers. The North Star. He breathed in deep and savoured the sweet earthiness of the vineyards. Then for a moment he thought of Gwen.

He heard rustling in the bushes and then the clink clinking of glasses before he heard Claude's muttering.

"Ah, there you are." He put the glasses down on a table, pulled up and sat on a lounger. "What are you looking at?"

"The stars. They're so clear and peaceful."

Claude looked up a moment. "This is one place in France where you can see them easily. There are no big cities. *Allors* no light pollution, no smog. Lots of pretty stars." Claude picked up the open bottle and poured two glasses. "*Salut.*" They toasted and drank.

Frank thought a few moments about the wine and said, "That's the most amazing taste."

Claude looked at him. "Very good; 1985 was a particularly great year here in Bourgogne. I will make a connoisseur of you yet. Maybe I can even find you a mission here in France where I can keep an eye on you and further your cultural education."

Frank laughed. "You're impossible."

"So are you."

They lay back, taking in the stars. There was silence save for the occasional hint of an automobile. At one point a car drove up the lane between them and the hotel, its motor silenced, then the sound of two doors and a trunk. *No threats in these sounds.* Then nothing. They could hear each other breathe.

More fabulous wine and glorious, peaceful silence.

At least fifteen minutes went by. Claude leaned forward to open another bottle. "You'll like this one." He smiled. "I know the owner." He poured.

"Claude, according to you everything from France is great, especially the wine."

"*Mais*, the years 1985, 1990 and even 1995 just happen to have been outstanding. Lucky for you, *mais oui*, France is still the greatest wine maker in the world." The more drunk Claude got, the more he slipped into his idioms.

Frank tried the wine. "A lot like the other one," he said, "just more … it's hard to describe."

"*Oui.*" Claude looked at him again. "And you are hard to understand. Have you ever really thought about why you do this work?"

"No." He knew that was a lie.

"Well then?" Claude probably knew it was a lie too. "You know, there is a new diagnosis people are talking about."

"What?"

"PTSD". He waited a moment. "Post traumatic stress disorder." He could hardly get the words out. "'Ave you thought about that?"

"No."

"Well, you should." Claude waited a moment. "You are a prime, as they say, candidate."

"Really?"

"*Oui.* Some of the things you have told me send the shivers up my spine. And I wasn't even there. But you…" His voice trailed off.

Frank thought for a moment, and decided to change the subject. He sat up and faced his friend. "When I was doing general surgery in Boston, it was like a stream of cases running together. You know what I mean. A gallbladder was a gallbladder. A hernia was a hernia. A colon was a colon. There were some technical challenges, and the teaching part was good, but after a while I felt like a revolving door."

"It's the repetitive nature of our work and our expertise with technicalities that makes us professionals!"

"I know. I know." He sipped some wine and reflected. "Then the trauma work—that was just a bunch of drunks, their victims and gunshots by gangs. The whole thing just ran together! Got me down."

"And?"

"Then Liz and I got into trouble…"

"Was there anybody else?"

"No. Nobody else. Not even one."

"Surely, *mon ami*, you could make things better—patch it up!"

"You're not married, Claude, you don't understand. You reach a point. A relationship reaches a point..." He sipped his wine. He shook his head. "You can't go back. And you know the Air Force in me started pulling. Where I am now, I feel I make a difference."

Claude sat there facing him in the dark, glass in hand, with his head cocked to the side. "I am sorry, *mon ami*."

"Don't be. I'm where I should be... where I need to be." He thought for a moment as he felt the wine and the hour. "I need to get to bed."

Claude got up with the bottles in one hand and his glass in the other. "*Moi aussi.*"

***

Driving back toward Mulhouse had given Frank a lot of time to think, although the state of his head made the whole thing a little difficult. When he wasn't thinking, driving the Porsche kept him firmly planted in reality. He needed to balance the power at the back with the feel of the steering against the palms of his hands in corners.

And Claude, his good if not best friend, whom he hadn't seen in over five years while he was self-absorbed in saving the world from itself, acted like a mother hen one minute and indulged him the next. Right up to the time they had breakfast by the pool that morning. Sending him away with a case of wine to share with Gwen, whom he didn't even know, as well as the special delivery of pills.

It occurred to Frank in the harsh shadow of daylight, driving as he was with a category three hangover, *Why do people bother with me anyway?* A valid question for Claude, the people in Boston, his wife, his children, Vern Carter. Only Gwen was in the thick of it with him. And her only recently. But Frank saw all of them on his terms. He called the shots. They waited.

Probably not good to go on this way in his mental state. *No!*

Without the afternoon glow of the sun, the beauty of the landscape he had seen the day before, escaped him.

He gave the car more juice and saw the speedometer climb to 290 klicks. He needed some diversion.

There was a piece of something red being blown across the road, like a piece of wrapper, thrown out of a car. He hit the brakes. Suddenly, in his mind's eye, it exploded into a giant jar of bubbling body parts, like in the operating room.

Panic stricken, he tugged right on the wheel to miss it. On the shoulder he tugged hard left, and mistakenly hit the throttle. The engine screamed and the car spun around twice. Coming to rest facing the opposite direction. Tires smoking.

A transport he hadn't even noticed was coming straight for him from behind. At the last moment, it veered to the left and missed him. It stopped in the middle lane with its flashers on.

The driver got out and ran toward him. *"Monsieur. Monsieur,"* he was shouting.

Traffic was passing by Frank on both sides, at speed.

He looked up and down the highway. There was nothing red left on the road

Frank thought a moment, but didn't know how he got this way. All he knew was that he had a hangover, and there *had* been something red. Perhaps it had blown away. Or, perhaps he had a problem—bigger than he knew.

Quickly, he convinced himself that everything was all right, even though he knew it really wasn't. He just couldn't connect the dots.

He had a quick chat with the transport driver and turned his car around. No more help was needed. Especially, not from the gendarmes.

He looked around again, and saw nothing red anywhere on the highway in either direction. There was a cross-wind.

Once in the car, he noticed the tremor in his hands as he tried to steady the wheel.

Mulhouse was just ahead. He let the speed drift down. The border appeared on the horizon. The lanes were empty.

He was directed to the left. He slowed more and more. The exhaust popped with backfire a few times.

He was waved into the main inspection station and came to a halt beside a green-uniformed border guard wearing a police cap and a side arm.

Frank lowered the window and handed the young blond man his passport.

The guard didn't say anything, didn't bend down to receive the document—let Frank strain to get it into his hand. The guard dispassionately looked over Frank with his blue eyes, glanced at the open passport, reached into his breast pocket for a whistle, which he quickly blew twice.

Two guards with submachine guns ran from the door of the blockhouse to the front and back of the car. They levelled their weapons at the windshields.

"*Aus machen! Fermé!*" the main guard ordered. Frank turned off the motor, and the guard went inside with his passport.

Damn! thought Frank. He had figured on sailing through the outside lanes with Vern's car. Here he was with a box of wine and a load of pills. Four thousand pills in the wooden box behind the seat, after less than one day in France. "Damn!" He was getting a headache. He was perspiring. He looked at his watch. Two minutes went by. Then five. Eight minutes. Frank had a feeling of impending disaster in his gut.

Finally the guard came out of the building, and with his right index and middle finger straight out, he motioned to and fro. The guards with the guns went back inside and Frank got his passport back.

"You can go!" he said curtly. He crossed his arms on his chest and stared down at Frank.

"A question?"

"*Ja.*"

"Why did you stop me?"

"This is General Carter's car." A thin smile came over his face. He leaned down. "You are not General Carter!"

TWENTY-FOUR

He had come to help with the evening mass, just as he had many times before. It was always a pleasure being back where he belonged.

It was tiring being around the sick and injured all the time. In fact, it saddened him that he wasn't able to do more, here.

When he really thought about it, and he had many times, he didn't understand why *he* had ended up this way. When so many of his brethren hadn't.

His belief was so profound, and he knew that he would never understand his longings completely. But even then, he hadn't been able to reconcile the two points of view.

He knew that the Lord worked in mysterious ways, and he wouldn't be able to understand his situation. Ever.

But none of this made it any easier.

His solution was to just not think about it anymore. When he did, it still left him with a feeling of bitterness and betrayal. Hurtful betrayal.

None of this was really on his plate. What was on his plate was a double espresso, as he was waiting for his ride home.

He felt good about the day. He had enjoyed the service.

Takes me home, to a better place.

There had been a time, before Father Andreas had communicated with him, that he felt ready to jump off a bridge. Except the coalition was blowing bridges up quicker than he could contemplate. All in the name of saving Sarajevo.

But sitting here, enjoying the late evening sky, at a sidewalk café— having a double espresso. That was good. No. That was great.

Especially after the early evening service.

Somehow, Father Andreas had heard that he was here. Not very far away. Perhaps he knew that he was lonely for the church. Or he just assumed so. It really didn't matter.

Andreas made it happen. He invited John to his church. To help him.

John knew that there was some advantage for Andreas, to him going. Who could resist the attraction of a visiting American priest? Especially here.

So John had been the second priest at all the Masses he had gone to. He had administered the eucharist, which Andreas called the badorak, because he was actually Armenian. Spreading the Pope's word in Bosnia.

John was perfectly happy with this. He would come when asked. Only when asked. Like there was still something there, holding him back, stopping him.

He came down with his robes packed in a tote, whenever he was asked. The vestments, that he had never given away. In spite of what had happened to him.

And how would Andreas know the truth? He wouldn't even consider enquiring at the Vatican, *Is Father John all right?*

They would reply, *Which Father John? Which diocese? When did he leave?*

Who else could Andreas ask?

Would they really, seriously know? Or would they just let things ride? Because as long as the money was coming in, who really cared?

The reality was that Father Andreas revelled in the fact that Father John was coming to help him.

And it swelled his ranks. The flock grew.

John was happy with the arrangement. He appreciated being back in the church. He loved getting away from the mission.

Like it's cleansing me, he thought, as he finished his espresso.

The only thing left to do was to wait for the transport to take him back up to the mission.

Father John looked at his watch. There was an hour left before he would get picked up. Just to be in civilization pleased him. What better than to have such a sweet evening after a service? To breathe the warm evening air and see the golden glow in the clouds.

A young girl came walking up the cobblestone. She had long, dark hair that fell on her shoulders. Deep brown eyes and some features of maturity. A young woman really.

She walked right past John and when she noticed how he was looking at her, she smiled.

He didn't recognise her from the church.

That fleeting smile woke something in John. There was a hunger in his soul and a burning in his loins. He felt a definite arousal. It was rare for a woman to affect him this way. Usually, he gladly waved them off. After his affair, John had developed other interests. But *she* could make his evening better. There had only been one other time since his transition that a woman had ever done this to him. Earlier on this mission, he had felt this way. Perhaps two months ago. And where did she end up but on his doorstep? Could have ratted him out!

All he could think of were her brown eyes looking at him and the perfect, dark hair, bobbing on her shoulders. Calling to him. *Come. Come get me.*

If he was going to win this girl, it had to happen fast. He threw enough Bosnian markas on the table to cover his tab, and then some. He didn't wait for change. He picked up his tote and set off, walking silently, stealthily behind the girl.

He looked around. There was nobody else on the street. They were nearing the edge of the village.

He felt his heart race.

John's shoe caught a stone on the gravel.

That made the girl look back and John noticed the surprise on her face.

But she didn't walk any faster, and he kept up his pace.

She turned around again and saw that he was still behind her. She started to run into the countryside.

That was her mistake.

John ran after her.

He ran harder than he could breathe, but caught up.

He grabbed her by the hair and pulled her down onto the ground.

The girl screamed.

TWENTY-FIVE

She had finished helping Dayna with the cleanup after breakfast. Then it was time for her to go to the village and get fresh food.

Over time, she had been given to undertake the task by herself. There had never been a problem. She had been certified to drive a troop carrier early in her army career. Jennifer drove the diesel truck with the blunt nose down the hill, and even got some pleasure from working the gears and hearing the engine whine.

She had put her pack in back of the driver's seat early in the morning. Before anybody else was up. Kitchen staff were the first to get up, and she opened before Dayna got there and started the food prep.

Jennifer didn't mind working for Dayna. Unless she was chiding her. But she never did figure out why Dayna did it. In fact, she liked her easy-going demeanor. So unlike regular army.

But neither of them were in the army any more. They were with an NGO. And Jennifer didn't have much money.

She thought about Dayna again. Maybe she sensed something in her. Or they were just never meant to really get along.

The big news was that Frank, the surgeon, was coming back later that day. Apparently with some new medication for the raped girls. Jennifer wondered if that could be of interest for her.

Might be something.

Jennifer had heard about the medication from Gwen, the bitch. Not like there was anything really wrong with Gwen. But she was a nurse. She had an actual career. She could go home and work in a hospital—not in a kitchen prepping food. Plus, she was sleeping with

Frank. Everybody knew that. Not that Jennifer was jealous. But just the sight of them; the skinny black nurse with the tall surgeon.

Doctors and their nurses. Nurses and their doctors.

She wondered what that would be like.

She was just getting to the left hand turn into the pine forest. Once in, the troop carrier was so big that it scraped bows on both sides.

Better focus on the job at hand. This was her first deal in Bosnia.

Jennifer couldn't remember when she first twigged to Miloje. They had always had a good and straightforward relationship. At first, she came down with Mike, the second duty sergeant, who was always smoking. He was there in case there was any trouble. But there never was, and so over time, he stopped coming.

In fact, there existed such a state of complacency with the locals, like there wasn't really a conflict going on at all. Just business as usual. She would come down and get the produce, vegetables, meat and dry goods, as well as any other consumables they needed. It was so much more reliable than the transports from Sarajevo. She always paid with Bosnian markas, which she got from Colonel Richter. The markas being safer than American dollars, which had a value in the local black market. She was safe carrying the Bosnian currency.

She remembered the first time Miloje said, *Is there something more I can do for you?*

Some weeks later he had said, *Maybe, there's something you can do for me.*

She let it slide, but she knew from that point, he was walking both sides of the street.

Perhaps he too, had seen something in her?

Over time, it became clear. Slowly, a dialogue developed. More like a dance with only a few steps at each meeting. An admission of this, a question of that. Never venturing too much at any one time. Until it became clear that he would be interested in some drugs.

She had asked him to be clear about what he needed.

He gave her a list.

The opportunity presented itself when the surgeon left for France. He would be gone for four days in total.

She did it, entering the clinic in a way only one person knew about—and he'd *never* tell.

Parking the troop carrier on the cobblestone street, she was ready. She had the knife in her pocket, in case anything went wrong. And she knew how to use it. Having been one of the first women in the army to undergo commando training. Until she was thrown out.

A sore spot with her because almost everybody there had *something on them.*

Why was I worse? Then, thinking about what was ahead, *Focus. Focus!*

She scooped up the pack and crossed the street to let herself into Miloje's store. She held it close to her side.

Miloje came out of the back room, showing his usual smile. But he must have felt something menacing in her stance, or in her expression. His look turned serious. Almost fearful. He said, "You give me package?"

"First the supplies," like she was issuing an order.

She didn't sense that there was anybody else in the back room.

They got the order together and placed it into cardboard boxes. She paid with Bosnian markas and got the receipt.

Miloje said, "Now you give me package?"

Her eyes gestured to the back room.

They went in and she put the back pack on his table. He opened it and spread the drugs across its surface.

As he opened the drawer, her grip tightened on the knife. If he did anything stupid, like pull a gun or a knife, she would slit his throat and dispatch him instantly. And deal with the consequences later.

He got out a paper and unfolded it. There was a list of drugs, with quantities and values attached.

As he reconciled the amounts with the prices, she did her own reckoning.

Miloje said, "I give eight hundred, American."

"That's worth at least twelve hundred."

"I don't have…"

"Don't fuck with me!"

He looked at her hand in her pocket, and must have known.

"I have maybe eleven hundred." His lips were quivering.

She rotated the grip on her knife.

He saw the action in her pocket, and said, "I show."

He went into another drawer and pulled out a tin box. He opened it slowly, cautiously. Not wanting to provoke.

There were different currencies inside.

He pulled out a bundle of American dollars from the bottom, held together by an elastic. Counting them out carefully, there were eleven hundred and forty-seven dollars, in various denominations. Mostly large bills.

Jennifer said, "That's good enough," and held out her left hand.

She stuffed the bills into her pocket. She wasn't going to over-reach for the other currencies and cause trouble. She would develop this relationship. Build on it.

He went to put the tin away.

She said, "Leave it." Wondering which drawer the gun was in.

They went out front.

Jennifer took her hand out of her pocket.

Miloje said, "Is good," and smiled, as if nothing much had happened.

They carried the boxes and her empty pack to the troop carrier together.

He waved as she drove off.

She thought, *Wonder why nobody else came in while I was there?*

TWENTY-SIX

Frank got back to the mission later that afternoon, with his Roots bag and two cardboard boxes. Gwen ran out to meet him at the dusty side of the truck.

She said, "Everything went well?" and hugged him.

"Yeah." He slung a cardboard box under one arm and hauled his bag with the other. He turned to the duty sergeant and gestured to the other box. "Take that pack to the clinic." He turned to her and said, "Got some supplies for the clinic."

They went to his quarters.

"So, take a look at this." He took a bottle out of the box.

"What is it?"

"A white Burgundy."

He got a corkscrew out of the cabinet, opened it and poured Gwen a small glass.

She sipped some. "Wow." After a moment she said, "We ought to chill the rest."

Gwen waited for him to open his leather bag. He got out the wooden box and put it on the table.

She slid the lid off.

"Oh my God. Look at this! All neatly packed in punch-out pockets." She stared at him. "How does your friend do this?"

"I told you. He's the guru from Boston. He's got pull." Frank poured himself a glass. "Hmm. Quite nice."

"You guys do a lot of this?"

"Afraid so."

"Can't say I blame you." She took another swallow. "Nice." She looked over to the box of wine and then at Frank, with questioning eyes.

He wondered if she was thinking about him in Rwanda.

There seemed to be a flurry outside. Frank went to the shuttered window. He pulled them up.

"I think that's Hradich's truck." He squinted to see. "It is. He looks angry. I think there's somebody in back."

Gwen came up beside him with her glass in hand.

Hradich went straight for their door. Running.

They went outside and met him.

Hradich was hyperventilating. "Come help. Is very bad. Come help."

As they ran to the truck, Richter was already outside.

There was a man in the back of the truck, ministering to a girl, lying on the floor who was sobbing uncontrollably.

They opened the back hatch..

"Oh my God," said Gwen.

Frank was speechless, taking it in.

The girl was wrapped in sheets, remnants of clothing hanging out. Her face had been beaten, swollen, her arms and legs cut. She was bleeding from the crotch. She was tall with long dirty blonde hair.

Frank turned to Richter. "Get a gurney." To Hradich. "What happened?"

The other man stammered the word out. "Rape."

"You her father?"

"Ya."

Hradich pacing in a circle. "I find, I kill. I find, I kill..."

"That's enough," Frank shouted at Hradich, as Richter and the duty sergeant came on side with the gurney.

Frank jumped into the back of the truck. "Help me lift her out." He picked up her legs.

The girl screamed in agony, hysterically pulling away from Frank.

Gwen was up by her head, trying to soothe her. Stroking her hair. "We're here to help you, sweetheart. We're here to help. What's your name?"

Her father said, "Is Irina."

Gwen kissed her forehead and said, "We're going to help you now. Lift you out, Irina. Take my hand, poor baby." She turned to Frank. "Go."

They swung her out of the back of the truck in one motion.

Irina screamed.

A few others of the mission staff had come out. Dayna stood there, eyes agog, hands over her mouth.

Richter steadied the gurney for them and peered into the truck's box. An expression of abject horror overcame his face. "*Ach du lieber,*" he gasped, seeing the pools of coagulated blood inside.

"Come on, come on," said Frank. "Let's get her in." On the way he said to Hradich, "You stay with Papa. Gwen and I will take care of this."

They got her in the room. Gwen was stroking her hair between cutting off the clothes and sheets.

Gwen turned to the drug locker, and said, "Oh no. Frank. We've been broken into!"

"What?"

"The drug locker's been broken into." She pointed to the drawer and looked in. "There's all kinds of stuff missing." She quickly rummaged through. "Mainly narcotics and antibiotics."

"Leave it. We'll deal with that later." His voice was pressured—angered. "There's fresh Ketamine and Versed in the box that I brought."

Gwen got the box from the duty sergeant's desk, and quickly sorted through it.

"Come on, Gwen. This girl needs help."

She turned to him. "I'm going as fast as I can. . ."

"I know you are. Just look at her." He was taking in the naked, bleeding, writhing young woman on the table.

Another nurse was soothing her.

Gwen came back with the drugs.

Frank loaded up some Versed and some Ketamine.

Gwen got a blood pressure cuff on her, pumped it up and said, "Blood pressure's good. Pulse one-fifty."

Frank had an IV in the other arm. He unloaded the syringes, and Irina fell silent.

An hour later, he had everything under control. He had cleaned her insides with hibitane and stitched the lacerations to her labia and vagina, as well as her arms and legs.

"Where do you want to go from here?" said Gwen.

"We wait until she wakes up and give her two pills. Then two more tomorrow." He looked at Irina a moment, lying oblivious on the operating table. He turned to Gwen. "Nature should reveal itself in a few days, with a nice period. We'll keep her here so we can watch her. I know you'll do a good job keeping her calm. Maybe we'll give her a few more hits of Versed? See if she develops amnesia for the whole thing."

Gwen peered over at Irina and said, "What kind of animal. . ."

"A human animal Gwen. A typically sordid, human animal." He rubbed her shoulder. "Same kind that steals your drugs." He turned to go, but looked back and said, "Don't say anything about the break-in until Hradich is gone. I'll inform Richter. I'm going to find Papa and Hradich. Inform them of our plan."

The other nurse said, "They're with Colonel Richter."

Probably into cognac or slivovitz.

As he left the clinic, he wondered whom he could trust any more.

***

Later when he was in his quarters, Frank got out his journal and remarked at how thick it was becoming. He recorded every detail of Irina's case.

TWENTY-SEVEN

Gwen and Frank were in Richter's office, that evening. The sunny glow from the tarpaulins over the windows was waning, giving way to the orange glow of incandescent light. All from a lamp on the colonel's desk. A look that made the room feel so much darker and more intimate, if that could be said of any colonel's office. At least it felt so much smaller.

Richter said, "I have never seen anything like that before. It's disgusting." He leaned forward, as if he was with friends. "How is she?"

"She's all right," said Frank, throwing a look at Gwen, who nodded. "We need to talk about a totally different issue."

"Not this again?"

"No. No, hear me out. We're talking about something completely different." Frank slowly looked over at Gwen.

She raised her hand slightly, shrugged, and said, "The clinic has been broken into." She turned to Frank, as if for approval.

"What?" Richter's chair protested. "What are you talking about?" His eyes darted from one to the other.

"I wanted to break this news to you, but now that Gwen has. Yes." The surgeon nodded. "The clinic has been broken into."

"What?" Richter shaking his head. "And—?"

"Drugs have been stolen." Frank was firm. He had done the counting with Gwen and the other nurse.

"Tell me."

"There was a break-in while I was gone. The drug locker was pried open, and drugs are missing. Mainly narcotics and antibiotics."

Richter left his chair with a protest, walked over to the door, throwing a moving shadow across the wall and bellowed, "Sergeant. Get up here."

They could hear, "Yes sir. Yes sir," between the footsteps on the stairs.

Richter held the door open, red faced and breathing heavily, as if he still felt the afternoon liquor.

The duty sergeant came in, looking bewildered. He saluted.

The colonel got right to the point. "What do you know of a break-in, at the clinic?"

"What? I mean pardon, sir. Nothing." He looked over at Frank and Gwen, and back at the colonel.

Richter pointed at Frank as they walked over to the desk. "Tell him."

Frank said, "When we were in the clinic today, with that raped girl, we saw what had happened. The clinic had been broken into."

"What?" The duty sergeant cocked his head.

Frank stood up and said, "The missing drugs are mainly narcotics and high-grade antibiotics." He let it sink in. "I guess we need to know who was in the clinic."

The duty sergeant seemed bewildered, eyes moving from one to the other. He said, "Nobody went in on my shifts. I don't recall Mike, uh, Sergeant Webber saying anybody went in."

"Well," Gwen ventured, "I didn't go in, *not once.*"

Frank shrugged his shoulders, "And I wasn't here."

Richter's quick stride toward the door was punctuated with, "Show me."

Moments later, the group was downstairs.

Richter had gone to the main door and shouted into the thin evening air, "Sergeant Webber."

The second duty sergeant joined them just as they were looking at the drug locker. A metal cabinet with individually lockable drawers. One drawer severely distorted around the lock, the tang bent but still sticking out.

Richter looked up from the near empty drawer and said to Webber, "What do you know of this?" He pointed at the drawer.

Webber, with an incredulous expression, said, "Nothing." He turned straight to Richter. "I had no idea."

"Did you see anybody go into the clinic?" Richter's voice was firm.

"Not a single one," said Webber. "There is only one way in and one of us is always there. From opening to closing. And then it's locked. Were the windows compromised?"

Gwen said, "I've already checked them." She shook her head. "Nothing."

Richter barked at Webber, "Check them again."

"Yes sir." He went for the windows.

"Not now." Richter was still red-faced, scowling his chevron, going to the front office. "First, we check the doors."

At the front door there was no sign of forced entry. No scratch. No scrape. Nothing.

It was getting dark, and they needed flashlights to examine the door locks and hinges. Richter seemed unhappy with that potential exposure. They were quick about it.

Richter led the group to the back room, past the gun lockers. He checked each locker's doors for security.

"Sergeant," he said to the first duty officer. "Open them up right now."

He had the key out from his ring in a moment and opened the lockers.

Rifles and pistols all in a row. Like they were on parade.

Richter checked two random samples of each for security. "Check the munitions."

The sergeant opened the ammo drawers and verified, "Nothing is missing sir."

Satisfied, Richter said, "Lock it up." He moved to the back room and inspected the door visually.

He opened it. The door didn't make a sound.

He switched the light on.

The storage room was without a window. There were boxes piled high, casting shadows from the solitary bulb in the ceiling. Nothing seemed disturbed.

Frank, Richter, and the sergeant went to the door.

It seemed untouched. The hinges and latch, an old type with a bar resting in a slot and a plunger below, somehow without blame.

Even the lock, a metal bar on a bolt that rested in a large slot on the door frame, seemed unscathed.

Richter unlocked the door, opened it, and ran the beam from his flashlight over the outside frame.

He said it all seemed well enough.

He closed the door and secured the locking bar.

Richter had nothing to say.

What nobody else had noticed, was the small ball of twine, about a centimeter in diameter, lying on the wood floor, beside a box of toilet tissue. Someone had discreetly kicked it to the edge of the box.

***

Colonel Richter was sitting alone in his office, after everyone had left, listening to the groan of his chair as he rocked back and forth. Thinking about how he would explain the drug theft. Who could he implicate?

Who would they think it could be? How do I write the report for UNPROFOR?

Someone from outside the mission was impossible. There were twenty-two people at the mission, including himself. Only a few had access to the clinic. Frank, three nurses, and the duty sergeants. Then there was the cleaning staff, who only went in when supervised by the duty sergeants.

He reached in his desk drawer and pulled out the cognac bottle and a glass. He poured a shot and held the glass up to the light, as if it might reveal something. But the alcoholic liquid only showed its burnt orange colour against the tungsten light.

A quick swallow didn't help either—didn't help him form a plan.

The colonel put the glass down and relaxed against the back of the chair, becoming a prisoner to his thoughts.

The most likely culprits in any case would be the three nurses. They had access but didn't go in while Frank was away according to both duty sergeants. He had heard about problem nurses before. They surprised the people around them when they were found out. Usually they had a bad habit that they needed to indulge. But in this case, antibiotics were missing too. More like a robbery for profit—which he knew it was. But he could play that like a cover-up.

However, he had no evidence, not even the slightest suspicion of any addicted staff that he could use. Not a single telltale sign, which he had seen before, on other missions. So there was nobody to implicate.

The people in these NGOs were always assumed to be clean. But a few were there because they had nowhere else to go. He knew that. Especially about Jennifer.

The second most likely group would be the duty sergeants. Easy access. No supervision. But it didn't fit. He knew these men from other missions. Never a problem, other than one being a little sloppy in his duties. Although, he supposed one of them could have helped someone that wasn't on his radar.

The cook wasn't even in the running.

Then there were Frank and Gwen. Both new to him. Both with unlimited access to the clinic. If he pressed it, what would their past reveal? Would it help him?

Either one of them could have gone in before Frank left. Jimmied the lock to make it look genuine, and taken the drugs. The duty sergeants wouldn't have noticed the barely open locker in the corner, if they went into the clinic. Which they said they didn't. And Frank left with a pack for Sarajevo on his way to Germany. In theory, he could have sold the drugs anywhere.

Luckily, the surgeon had come back with a fresh box of drugs. Narcotics, antibiotics and more. All properly signed for and delivered.

Coincidence? Or could he deliver that story another way if he had to?

Richter would file his report to UNPROFOR in the morning. See what their impression was. He knew there was no point in searching the buildings. He knew, and everybody else in the mission knew, the drugs were long gone and a search would only create bad feelings. Reduce morale. And for what—a show? *My show?*

No. He would leave things alone and see what his superiors had to say. Let their response guide him.

Richter would have to be extra vigilant. He would put some new procedures and protocols into place. Make it look like something was being done.

The real problem was, who would trust him?

Frank and Gwen?

He struggled with his dilemma for some time, and finally gave up.

Everything would resolve itself. It always did.

He got up and let himself out. The duty sergeant was long gone. He locked the door and quickly crossed the square, coming to the side of the three buildings that housed the officers. Better to be near a building than to be walking in the middle of the square.

Frank occupied the first building, a small one, by himself. It was dark.

Likely in bed with Gwen, asleep.

The second had two entrances. One for Father and one for him. The third had one entrance and was occupied by the sergeants. There were more buildings down the row.

In the light before moonrise, the rough outer stone walls gave up craggy monstrous faces that hid in the contours.

He came upon Father John's window and noticed the light was on inside. He cast a glance sideways, through the partly open shades, and saw Father John. Richter stopped out of curiosity.

The priest was pacing back and forth, his ceremonial shawl draped around his neck, falling onto his undershirt. He was reading frenetically from the bible in his left hand.

Richter couldn't make out what he was saying. He stole closer to the window.

He could only make out two words, mercy and forgiveness.

Better leave before someone accuses me...

Poor Father, he looks tortured.

TWENTY-EIGHT

Monday came, and so did Hradich.

Frank had seen him race up the road.

Fortunately for Irina, Sunday had come with a period. A big, heavy period. And she actually smiled. Gwen showered her and paid her lots of attention. Lots of hugs and girly talk. And meals.

As for Frank? He had given Irina a few more shots of Versed. *Necessity, the mother of invention.* And he had wondered what Irina thought of Gwen.

Since he had covered her with major antibiotics, for all the lacerations, they were now running low again. In spite of what he had brought up from Sarajevo. The supply just wouldn't last.

Hradich's focus was different. "You have girls here."

Babic had dropped off five more.

Frank said, "Yes. There are girls from another village."

"Why I do not know?"

"They're from far away."

"*I* am UN." His voice was pressured. "Why, *I* do not know?"

"I thought you did," Frank lied. "There are other leaders that bring them here." He thought Hradich's expression cooled.

"Ya." Like he wasn't even seeing Frank while staring right at him. So absorbed. "I understand."

But Frank, sensing the disconnect, didn't think so. "Kamenko," he said, "I have to serve all the people, and all the children of Bosnia Herzegovina. Not just you." He paused and shrugged. "Some of these people you simply don't know."

Hradich stared at him with an empty expression.

Frank put his arm on Hradich's shoulder, trying to soothe him. "I have to tell you something. I've been to France. To pick up some medicine."

Hradich pulled his shoulder away and glanced at him.

"Irina is the first girl I've given the medicine to. So. I didn't have to operate to take away the rape."

Hradich stopped and faced him, like he was just waking up. "Why you not operate? Is better, no? I bring you good willow stick."

"Kamenko, this medicine works well, if the girl has just been raped. If she has just been raped in the last day or two, we can give her the medicine."

"Then, why I bring you stick?" His hands held up as he pivoted away.

"Because there will always be other girls who were raped weeks ago. Those I will have to operate on." He let it sink in. "And honestly, we were running out of supplies. Plus, Gwen and I couldn't keep up." He knew the next would be the hard part. "There are more people here than just you who need us to fix their girls."

Frank immediately regretted using those two words *Just you*. He hoped they would evaporate.

"So, from now on," said Frank, "if you have a girl recently raped in the last day or two, you bring her here right away. I'll fix it with medicine. If it happened three days or more, we'll have to operate."

Hradich seemed to take the whole thing in stride for a change. He appeared to be mulling it over. He turned and paced a bit.

He said, forcefully, "How many other girls you have?"

Surprised, Frank answered, "Five. And five more for Wednesday."

The whole conversation had taken place outside the door to Frank's quarters. Fortunately, nobody had come along to hear what they were saying. At least, Frank thought, it was better that way. He also knew

Gwen was getting the girls ready for their procedures, so he couldn't stay too much longer.

Hradich stood with an expression on his face that Frank could only describe as defiant.

"I have five girls too," said Hradich finally. "When *I* can bring?"

Frank was amazed at the lack of humility. Not even a, *my friend, can you fix?* Just straight to the question. Like a foregone conclusion.

He said, "Bring them on Thursday afternoon."

"Okay. I bring," said Hradich. "I need to talk colonel."

With that he turned and walked away.

TWENTY-NINE

The week came and went. Frank lay in bed thinking about everything that had happened.

They had done Babic's girls without any hitches. The first five were especially animated, talking all the time. As if nothing was wrong. Frank thought about that, every time he watched the glass jars on the wall fill with bloody remnants.

On Tuesday, he had a conversation with Richter.

"We're low on antibiotics again. We need to get some more."

"Unfortunately, the road to Sarajevo isn't passable. Mined." Richter made a throwaway gesture from his creaky rocker. "Looks like you were just plain lucky to get out when you did." He paused, like he was thinking about their situation. "And to get back in with what you brought. Besides, I thought more antibiotics were supposed to come back with you on the truck."

"Surprised the heck out of me too. We got all our medical supplies and disposables, plus the drugs that they gave me. Which wasn't much. I asked, but they said that was our consignment. Maybe they need them in Sarajevo." Frank thought a second. "Or they just plain forgot." That was much more likely.

"How military of them." Richter chuckled. Then he became very serious. "Frank. I have to tell you something." He leaned forward. "Remember we were talking about a war—a genocide, you said."

"Yes."

"It seems that *I* was wrong. UNPROFOR has let it be known that a mass grave has been found about fifty kilometres east of here."

"Really?"

"All men and boys." He went for the brandy in the bottom drawer. "Some of them not even shot…"

Frank wriggled his hand like he had a glass with cubes in it. "Remember when we went to the village and the bridge got taken out?"

"Ya." Richter poured two glasses and pushed one across the table.

Frank took a pull, remarked at how good it was, and said, "I never told you about this. But Gwen knows."

"What?"

"The water in the gutters ran red. Do you remember that?"

"Ya. The soil."

"No. I tested it when we got back. It was blood."

Richter cocked his head. "And you didn't tell me about it?"

"I discussed it with Gwen; but we figured it would be dismissed as blood from an animal slaughter, for a market." Frank took another pull of the brandy. "Besides, there was no way of proving it was human blood out here."

"But you should have told me about it."

Frank considered how he was going to say it. "Sir, I didn't think you were in the mood to listen."

*⁂

Babic picked up his girls on Tuesday and dropped off five more. They were orderly and friendly but didn't have the charisma of the previous bunch.

Babic picked them up on Thursday morning. Nothing unusual there.

Hradich didn't show up with his girls until late Thursday afternoon, which was unusual for him. Frank had thought that maybe he didn't want to see the other girls, or know who had brought them. Or…

maybe he just didn't want to be seen by Babic or his girls. All very strange for Hradich, who had always been so in everyone's face.

Then he picked them up on Saturday. Not staying long.

Now Frank lay in bed on his back, with Gwen curled over his left side. She was softly purring, almost snoring in his ear. Her short pubic hair scratched his left thigh with every breath.

There was nothing scheduled for Monday. Neither Hradich nor Babic had indicated any need for abortions. And they both knew that the pills were available for fresh rapes.

Frank wondered what the week would bring. Would either of the men pick up on acting promptly with early rapes? If they did, would they bring in the girls on time or would they dither? Procrastinating because they were familiar with the results of the procedure and not completely sure of the effects of the pills. Or would they choose to ignore Frank altogether?

And then the ultimate question: Were they on opposite sides of the conflict?

That's not good, if it's true.

But at least the UN, well not the UN, but UNPROFOR, had reported the mass grave. And Richter had conceded that Frank was right. And if Hradich *was* the UN Liaison, why had he become so cool?

Frank wondered whether the UN would ratify the findings of its military force in Yugoslavia to the rest of the world. Or would they procrastinate and stretch UNPROFOR with unreasonable demands and untenable rules of engagement, like they had done in Rwanda.

If they do that, it won't be good for us.

Frank wished he had some kind of a crystal ball. But he didn't.

Gwen shifted closer, and her hand clutched him lightly.

On top of all that, the drug theft still troubled him. Even though he had seen it before on other missions. There was always someone. He decided to dismiss that thought. He sighed and fell into a troubled sleep.

THIRTY

"You bastard!" She took a swing at him, screaming. "Get Out!"

He pressed his foot in the door. Liz was strong. He hoped the neighbours couldn't hear. "Liz," he pleaded, half wanting to whisper, half wanting to shout. "Liz?" He pushed harder on the door, hoping it wouldn't break. Finally making headway, the door opening wider.

"Get out!" Shrill. "Leave us alone! You don't live here!"

Frank pushed in.

He caught a fist to his temple, then one on his mouth. He pushed back. Felt his heart race. Careful not to hit.

"Get out! Get out!"

He got in.

She turned and ran down the hall to the kitchen, her head of long blond hair bobbing with every step. She scooped up their son, Joshua, who had been sitting in his playpen, mouth wide open, and held him close in front of her like a shield.

Frank stopped in the doorway, one hand resting on the frame, panting. "Put him down!"

"Get out!" She pointed to the door with her right hand. "Get out!" Her voice was so shrill that Joshua turned toward her and started to cry.

"You're not going to hide behind him." He approached her. "He's my son too!"

"Don't come near me, you *bastard!*" She spat the words. "You get the fuck out of here and don't ever come back."

They turned in the centre of the kitchen like two cagey fighters in the ring.

"You think you can keep pulling this off? Think you can treat us this way?"

Frank was pleading again, "It's what I *do*."

"No! No, it's not. It's what you *want* to do…"

"Liz. Honey…"

"Don't call me 'honey.'" She shook her right fist at him. "Don't you dare call me 'honey.'" Joshua was wailing, dangling in her arm on her left hip.

"*It's what I do!*" When I'm on call…"

"That's what's wrong with you. You're always on call. On call for somebody *else*. While we sit here and wait, you're taking care of somebody else. You do it well."

"Honey…"

"Shut the fuck up! Just shut up and listen." She jabbed at him twice. He backed off. Her eyes were dilated, red with rage. "I've been waiting for you for years. *For years!* We've been waiting for you for years. But you know what?" She paused as she spun around. "We don't matter."

Frank half expected the police to show up. *Oh, boy. Not that.* He wanted to speak. Calm her down. But she wouldn't let him. He kept himself facing her as she danced around.

"You know what happens? Work gets the best part of you. We get what's left over! We get the broken-down asshole who drags himself home, too tired to talk. Who's fed up and wants a private solitude. Well, you're going to get your own private solitude when you're out of here! And we're moving on. Moving on to a normal life."

That was it! Frank had it. Had it good! He moved in.

"You stay away from me. Don't touch me!"

In one quick motion he nabbed Joshua out of her arms. That made him cry louder. He quickly bent down to sit him in his playpen.

Liz was beating him around the head. "See what you did to him, you bastard!" One blow caught his right ear and hurt real bad.

Frank turned around and repelled her. "He's my son too! He's my son too!"

"Oh, yeah? We'll see about that!" She lunged at him. He caught her by the arms. "Let go! Let go of me!" She writhed in his arms, starting to kick now. "Let go. Let go! I'll tell everybody what you did to me."

He wished he could calm her down.

She kicked him in the right shin, cutting through his pants.

"Owww…" He bent down to see.

Hands loose, she clasped them together and smashed her fists up into his face.

He stumbled back and hit the wall.

She beat him on the chest.

Frank was fainting. Going down.

There was tugging at his right arm. Heart racing. He was coming back but couldn't see clearly. There was a dark face sitting across from him. It was slowly taking shape.

"Frank." Softly. Then agitated. "*Frank!*"

He recognized Gwen's voice, and she finally came into focus.

"Frank. What happened?" She gently rubbed his free hand in hers. "Where were you just now?"

He looked down at his right hand. The one clutching a coffee mug. Most of the contents spilled all over their tabletop in the canteen.

Frank looked at her. "What?"

"It's like you were here one moment and gone the next." Gwen said, "I couldn't make out what you were saying." She was clearly disturbed. "What set you off?"

Frank looked around the canteen. What he could see was emptiness. He turned in his chair and looked over the rest of the room. There was only Dayna behind the counter, throwing him the odd glance.

He turned squarely to Gwen. "I don't know."

THIRTY-ONE

Monday came as a day without an agenda.

There were no abortions to do. No pills to hand out. There wasn't even the remotest sign of an injured villager. But there never had been.

Richter had mused at breakfast that perhaps the mass grave finding was in error, because New York hadn't endorsed UNPROFOR's findings.

Which had only made Frank think of General Carter's comments about NATO.

Jennifer served them this morning.

Frank noticed how Richter had watched her approach the table, and his smile.

She had left them to eat, without saying a word.

So it was the first Monday in weeks that Frank felt like setting up a chair in the sun out back of his quarters and soaking up some rays, in spite of the warnings about snipers. After all, they had never received a single shot.

Gwen had gone off earlier to do a supply inventory with the duty sergeant. New rules.

Without her there, he had abandoned his reserve and was sprawled on a comfortable reclining chair, shielded from everybody's view behind his quarters, with nothing on but a pair of shorts, feeling the gentle sting of the Mediterranean sun. Not like the summer sun, but still deeply soothing.

He revelled in the beauty of the rolling hilltops all around him, decorated with the odd stand of trees. A sky that was clear and yet wasn't. A gentle mist almost imperceptible, taking the edge off distant features.

Must be the ocean.

And more, how could war come to such a beautiful land? Much less a racial action. But he knew the logic to these things was always horribly flawed.

And if there was a sniper out there—*Let him take me out. 'Cause I'm the only surgeon between here and Sarajevo.* He chuckled.

All thoughts that comforted Frank until he heard the distant sound of the car's engine. It sounded like Babic's.

He was inside and changing in a moment, covering up. When the car entered the square, he walked out his door, fully clothed.

Gwen came out the main building with Richter.

Babic's truck came to a dusty halt in the square. He was out in a moment, walking toward Frank.

He stopped in front of him, and said, "I have two girls, need you help."

Frank saw the urgency in his eyes and said, "Yes?"

He gestured toward the truck. "Two girls raped yesterday."

Frank turned to Gwen, then the truck, and finally at Babic. "Bring them inside."

Babic opened the door of the truck, said something in Yugoslavian, and the girls got out.

Frank motioned to the main building.

The two girls dutifully followed Babic, shuffling a few steps behind him. Both were dressed in black, with kerchiefs on their heads, looking down somberly.

He watched them until they were almost in the door. Then he joined Gwen.

As they walked over, she said, "They seem kind of genuine to me."

"I agree," said Frank as they walked in the heavy wood door.

Once in the clinic, Frank started the questioning, and Gwen took notes. "When did this happen?"

Babic relayed the questions, and interpreted the answers for the first girl. She was raped yesterday. Mid-morning.

Esma, the second girl, understood English and answered for herself. "Just before ten o'clock, yesterday night."

"Where did it happen?"

Some talk back and forth, and Babic said, "Behind a ruined farm near our village."

Esma said, "Strange men drive car beside me in town. Pull me into car and drive to farm east of our village. One man throw me on ground. Pull up my skirt. Pull down my pants and force himself in me. I scream, but nobody comes. Other two men do the same."

Frank thought she seemed quite composed. "Is this the first time?"

"Ya, but happen to my friend. Five men. She has baby!" Esma looked around at them. "I not want baby."

Frank thought a moment. "I should examine you both."

There was some talk between Babic and the girls.

Finally Babic said, "Is good." He glanced at the two of them. "You examine."

"All right then." Frank turned to Gwen. "Get them ready."

She said, "Yes, *sir*," and set into the task with a polished efficiency.

Frank got to the first girl, who was gowned and on a gurney, Gwen holding one hand and cradling her head. It was the same drill. Legs bent. Heels and knees together. Let the knees fall apart. Breathe deep a few times. Pull the sheet up and insert the well lubricated speculum.

"Ah!" The first girl squirmed.

Gwen whispered in her ear.

She fell silent.

Frank adjusted the light and peered inside, spreading the speculum slowly.

"Ow…"

Frank registered the details quickly. He rotated the speculum on the way out to see the full sides of her vagina.

"Ah…" as the speculum slid out.

She was badly bruised, and her hymen was in bloody tatters. *She'd been a virgin.* Frank noted the details on her chart.

He pointed to her clothes and nodded to her with a smile so that she'd get dressed.

"Ready for the next one?" he said to Gwen.

"Yes, *sir.*" She was keeping up appearances. She gave the girl a hug and walked her over to the change curtain.

Once again, the same drill. Esma yielded and moaned when the speculum went in.

Gwen comforted her, and it was right then that Frank realized how good she had been with all the girls. He'd write that into her performance review.

Esma was very bruised at her entrance and all up the sides of her vagina. *Must have struggled hard.* She had no hymen.

Once they were dressed, the four went out to meet Babic in the duty room. Babic was holding his hat. Nobody was paying any attention to the duty sergeant.

"All right," said Frank. "The girls obviously need help. We'll get them the pills, and we expect them to have a normal period a day or two after they finish the pills."

Babic said, "What is period?"

"Bleeding in pants," said Gwen. "Girl bleeding every month."

"Oh, ya." Babic shrugged.

Gwen dug into her pockets and got out the punch packs of pills.

"You take two now and two tomorrow," said Frank.

The duty sergeant gave them glasses of water.

The girls punched out two pills each and washed them down.

"Do you have our other package?" Frank said to Gwen.

"Right here." She pulled out two small medication envelopes.

"This is an antibiotic," said Frank. "Try to prevent gonorrhea and syphilis."

"Ya," said Babic.

Obviously, he knows what those are.

On the way over to his truck, Babic said, "Thank you, doctor," and shook Frank's hand. He turned to Gwen. "And to nurse, thank you." He shook her hand too.

The midday sun was getting hot and cast narrow shadows. There was animated conversation before Babic's group left, leaving nothing behind but their tire prints in the square.

Frank thought he heard another vehicle approaching. It crested the rising grade into the compound, just after Babic had driven out.

The driver of the pickup truck had his head turned back, looking behind him at the departing truck. He stopped just in time to avoid hitting anyone.

Frank could barely make out the driver at first. But when he got out, it was clearly Hradich, and the expression on his face was one of disdain.

Hradich softened his approach as he walked up to Gwen and Frank. He said, "I bring you one girl. Rape yesterday. You fix."

Not a question, thought Frank. Resigned to the new order with Hradich, he said, "Sure. Bring her in."

Hradich waved at the door. It opened, and a tall slender girl of about seventeen stepped out, holding her head down.

Gwen walked over and put her arm around the girl's shoulder, guiding her across the square to the clinic. Svetlana was taller than Gwen.

Inside the clinic, the same things happened all over again.

This girl was even more sensitive than either of the others before her.

"Ah, ah, ah…" and she started to cry when Frank inserted the speculum.

Gwen was barely able to control her.

Frank got a good look. She was badly bruised, inside and out. No hymen. He noted it in her chart.

Then he realised that Hradich had not responded to her crying. Not one little bit. Not like he did with Zivka. But then maybe he was getting desensitized too by the sheer volume of the rapes.

Svetlana was given her pills and her instructions, as well as the antibiotics. All with Hradich passively looking on.

Frank decided to engage him. "How's Zivka?"

"Is good." He didn't look directly at Frank. He didn't betray any emotion.

"Well, I'm glad to hear that." Frank was expecting something more.

But Hradich simply pointed the way out of the room and walked with Svetlana to his truck. She let herself in and closed the door.

"Bye, Kamenko."

"Bye-bye."

Frank thought he detected that scowl again, but just barely, as Hradich got in the Toyota pickup.

The engine turned over and they were gone in a swirl of dust.

"Kinda makes you want to give them a thousand pills and tell them to go to hell, doesn't it?

Gwen looked at him a moment and said, "What are you doing now?"

"Think I'm going to lie down." Knowing full well it was a lie.

"I'm going to finish the inventory."

"See you for supper."

They parted.

Once in his quarters, Frank undressed to his shorts. He went to the cupboard and poured himself a couple of inches of slivovitz. He drained a little pull and did his journal entry. Satisfied he picked up his towel and went out back to his reclining chair. He spread out the towel and balanced the slivovitz on the arm of the chair.

Lying back, he pulled down his sunglasses and picked up where he had left off. The roundness of the hills. Those trees. The Mediterranean haze. And the stinging warmth of the sun on his pale skin. All conspiring to make him feel good.

He sat up and drank some more. *This shit can grow on you.* In a few minutes he had drained the glass.

Frank went back inside and poured himself a few more inches. The bottle was almost empty.

He was thinking about the brandy when he sat back down outside. Hradich hadn't brought any more. Of course, he had wine. But that was to drink with Gwen. What should he do? Drop Hradich a hint? Ask him to pick some up? Give him some money to pick some up? Try to get it through the supply routes, which were down? Get Jennifer to pick some up on a supply run? Somehow that didn't appeal either.

He'd figure it out.

Frank sipped and looked around at the rolling hills. He smiled. Then the Adriatic coast came to mind. The craggy white coastline lapped at its edges by the azure blue of the Mediterranean. He had been there once. That, with the warmth of the sun and the burn of the slivovitz, should have given him some comfort. But wherever he turned, it was the scowl on Hradich's face that he saw, etched over the beautiful background.

✳✳✳

Father John woke up soaked in perspiration.

It was as if he was in a bed of water, the sheets clung to him. The mattress, one of those quilted old world lizards stuffed with cotton, was in danger of becoming a rusty lizard. How could his body betray him this way?

There was only one thing on his mind. Original sin. Not the sin of being born… That had been forgiven… He had been baptized…

His original sin. The one that had taken him down this path.

He sat up. Threw off the sheets. The breezes let in by the leaky windows cooled and dried the skin on his back. Then, as if they were caressing him, they moved around to his chest as he turned. He felt so much better that he had got up, and felt his buttocks to peel off his damp bottoms.

Leaning heavily onto his palms on the small table as it creaked in protest, he thought about Gail.

He wanted to pray.

But all he could think of was being on top of her. Inside her. Spending himself in her.

Even though she was married to one of his parishioners.

His right hand came up and rubbed his eyes and the bridge of his nose.

He saw her in front of him as if she was right there. Beautifully naked in his rectory bedroom. He adored everything about her. Except that she was married.

But she had revelled in their sin too. She had made him so hard he didn't even recognise himself.

When the time had come for her to depart, he had looked at himself in the mirror, wearing his collar once again.

My mirror broke for me that day.

He realized now that he hadn't been able to look at himself critically in a mirror for some time.

He should have gone to confession. But…

Then the boys…

Much later, those pieces of mirror, swept under a carpet by my bishop. The one who wouldn't hear my confession.

He turned the light on. Got his ceremonial shawl out of his footlocker, put it around his neck, and held the bible in his left hand.

He said, "Forgive me, Father, for I have sinned."

But he knew he couldn't take his own confession. He would need another priest for that. Father Andreas?

After what he had done in the village?

Father Andreas could hear him confess about Gail. At least that would be a start.

How would I end it with Andreas? There's so much more.

He would have to wait until he was back in the States to confess to the rest.

That might work. He could travel a bit and find a sympathetic ear here or there.

A good plan for now.

On the other hand, what's the use of confessing when you love the fruit of your sin?

He was even more confused, pacing back and forth, leafing through the new testament, wondering what verse might bring him comfort.

The bible trembled in his hand. The solitary, dim bulb amplified his motion on the far wall.

Father John said quietly, "Forgive me, Father…"

THIRTY-TWO

Gwen woke up first. She was moving and shifting in bed.

Frank registered the change before he even woke up. When he did, it was like the continuation of a dream. Just not one of his nightmares.

Gwen was folded in half, massaging her ankle. She started to mutter.

"Damn."

Frank rolled over and looked at the shuttered window. It was light outside. They had slept in.

"Jesus Christ," she said. Rubbing her ankle harder. "Ow…"

Frank rolled back toward her. "What's the matter?"

"My spot hurts."

She rubbed it some more and began to reposition herself.

"What's wrong?" he said.

"You smell like booze." Her look pierced him.

Finally, she pulled her side of the covers back and straddled Frank, naked, to get out of bed.

Frank watched her weaving a path to the bathroom. He heard her pee. Then he heard the water run. A long moment went by. She came out the door and stopped. Looking in shock, with her arms hanging.

"Frank…" she screamed.

"What's the matter?" He was fully awake. He pivoted out of bed and hurried over to the bathroom.. "What's the matter?"

Gwen was tearing up. "Loo… look at my ankle."

Frank bent on his knees. He stared at her ankles.

"The left one. On the inside."

He looked at it carefully and thought he saw a large skin pore.

"Get over on the bed," he said.

They went over. He moved the white table closer and turned on the lamp. With Gwen lying down, he examined it carefully. There was what looked like a large pore in the incandescent light. Right on the inside knuckle of her ankle. He let his gaze go up her bare legs and torso, to her face, as he gently pushed on the pore.

"Ahhh…" She moaned and writhed.

Frank looked at it again. "Sorry."

There was a drop of fluid working its way out of the pore.

Frank caught it with a tissue and examined it under the table lamp. A smudge of yellow fluid and puss.

The worst came to mind.

"Gwen, how long has this been going on?"

"A few weeks. You know. Since I told you in the clinic room. It's just never been this bad."

He sat on the bed beside her and massaged her thigh.

"What do you think?" She had her hands covering her mouth.

He thought about it. "I don't feel a lump, and it's not warm. There's puss and serous fluid." He turned to her. "Not a skin abscess. My worry is osteomyelitis."

"Oh shit," she shouted. She hammered the bed once with both fists. She propped herself up on her elbows. "What are we going to do?"

"We don't have a bone scanner. We don't even have X-ray." He turned to her. "But it's just my hunch."

"Frank, we have to do something."

"I'll … We'll talk to Richter." He knew they were in a pickle, but he didn't want to alarm Gwen any more than he had to. She was upset enough. Besides, she had probably come to the same conclusion. Only she wanted to know what he thought. "We'll talk to him as soon as we can. Come on, let's get dressed."

***

They were sitting in Richter's office, in the green leather chairs facing his desk. It was a clear day. The tarpaulin over the window to his right, was glowing orange brown with the bright sunlight. Richter kept the tarpaulins over his windows twenty-four-seven. A routine precaution for a career military man in sniper country.

"And what is the matter," he said from behind his desk.

"It's Gwen," said Frank, glancing her way. "She has a problem with her ankle."

"Really," said Richter, placing both of his hands on his desk and pushing his chair back to partially recline. "What exactly is the problem?"

"The problem is that she seems to have an infection of the bone on the inside of her ankle." Frank waited for his answer.

"And how do you know this?" Richter looked deadpan at Gwen. He turned back to Frank and shrugged. "She seems quite well."

"Exactly," said Frank. "I'm basing the diagnosis on my physical exam and Gwen's history." He wondered if Richter's attitude toward them had been tainted by the stolen drugs.

"I bumped it into a gurney in the clinic a few weeks ago," said Gwen as she leaned forward in her chair.

"I see," said Richter.

"The spot on the ankle is quite small," said Frank. "In fact, it's like a large pore, with body fluid and puss coming out."

Richter pivoted his oak chair forward, propped himself on his elbows, and peered over the desk at Gwen's ankle.

She everted her left ankle and pulled her pant leg up so Richter could see.

"That's a very small bandage," said Richter. "The problem you are describing is very serious." He turned from one to the other. "How can you be sure? Don't you need some tests?"

"That's why you're the camp commandant," said Frank. "What we need is an X-ray and a bone scan of the ankle."

"And. . ." said Richter as he turned up his palms.

"The closest place with those services is in Sarajevo," said Frank. "When do you think we can go?"

Richter crossed his arms on his chest and held his chin with his left hand. "That presents a problem."

"Don't tell me," said Frank.

Gwen was getting visibly upset.

"UNPROFOR reports that the main roads between here and Sarajevo are once again mined." Richter let it settle in. "Your transport back was the last to get through. It will be at least a week before we get the roads cleared. As I told you before, there is a civil war going on. That war has not yet been officially recognized by NATO in New York."

"Well, isn't that the cat's meow." Frank stood up and started to pace. "The problem is we need antibiotics for Gwen, and we're getting low on that."

"The antibiotic order was partially completed on the last transport," said Gwen. "We barely have enough for the girls, but I need something different. Right, Frank?"

"Yeah." He walked over to Richter's desk. "We need Cipro and clindamycin. Enough to last at least a month."

"Let me write it down," said Richter, looking concerned. "You know I will do what I can."

Frank spelled out the names and the doses.

"I will message UNPROFOR today and let you know their response."

∗∗∗

They were in Richter's office again, only now it was late afternoon. The tarpaulin to Richter's right looked dead, but the one behind him radiated its orange optimism into the room.

He said, "I have contacted UNPROFOR headquarters at the Sarajevo airport. I'm afraid the news is not good."

Gwen lowered her head.

"There is no way a transport or any other vehicle will get out of Sarajevo on these roads. There is no other place nearby for an X-ray, let alone a bone scan."

Frank was getting ready to speak, but Richter held up his hand.

"And," he said, "there is no way for UNPROFOR to get drugs up here." He held his hand out toward Frank. "Flying anything up here would be suicide. You remember the village of Serdansk? Well, apparently the surface-air missile radar is crackling and popping. So that is a no-go."

Frank was getting desperate. He turned to Richter. "Maybe we can ask Hradich to help. He knows his way around."

Richter looked at Frank for a long moment, and said, "I'll get him up here tomorrow."

Frank turned to Gwen and felt his heart sink.

*⁎⁎⁎

After supper in the canteen they went to his quarters and had some wine at the little table. Later, Frank changed the bandage on Gwen's ankle and saw more puss and fluid come out of the pore-sized hole. For a moment, he felt powerless—demoralised.

THIRTY-THREE

Hradich arrived in a flurry and a cloud of dust in the main square within an hour of Richter calling for him.

They were sitting in Richter's office in the comfortable glow off the east window's tarpaulin. Hradich had put his beret on the arm of the leather chair, and his AK-47 leaned up against the side.

Richter said, "Doctor Lambert has something he needs to ask of you."

Hradich turned to Frank, who was beside Gwen on a wood chair. "What you need?"

"First," said Frank, "how's Svetlana?"

"Is fine." Hradich looked dispassionate.

Frank quickly glanced at Gwen in the green leather chair beside him before saying, "Gwen has been injured. We need your help."

Hradich betrayed some disbelief when he looked at Gwen. "I am Liaison. Not doctor. What I can do?"

Frank knew she still looked well. No obvious discomfort. Groomed impeccably, as always.

Richter leaned forward and said, "We are having some problem since the war was declared."

Hradich cocked his head and said, "Nobody bothers you."

"You are right about that," said Richter. He shifted uncomfortably in his chair, making it creak. "But we can't get supplies." He raised his eyebrows. "Because the roads are mined and the SAM missiles are all active."

"Is stupid," said Hradich, holding up his palms and turning from Richter to Frank and back again. "When UN was police action, you do what you want. You bring NATO jets. You bomb bridges." He paused a moment. "Now is war. You do nothing." He wore an incredulous expression, turning in the leather chair from Richter to Frank, back and forth.

"You are right," said Richter. "It takes the UN time to decide what it will do." He looked at Frank and shrugged.

Frank thought he knew what Richter must be thinking.

"So," Richter pronounced it his German way, "why don't you explain to the Liaison what you need, Doctor."

"Nurse Pakin has an infected bone in her left ankle," Frank said to Hradich.

Gwen pulled the leg up on her fatigues and turned the inner part of her ankle to Hradich.

There was the beige bandage on the black skin of her inner ankle.

Hradich leaned forward and squinted. "Is not big."

"But it's very serious," said Frank. "It will fester, and Gwen could lose her leg. I have no tests, no X-ray, because we can't leave. I make this diagnosis from what I see."

"I believe. I trust. You are good doctor." There wasn't the slightest hesitation in his voice.

Somehow those words were lost on Frank. But he added, "Can you get us to Sarajevo or another big city where we can get X-rays and other tests?"

Hradich shook his head. "No. Is too dangerous to go to big city. Too much fighting."

Frank wondered why he didn't mention the mined roads. "Then can you get us some medicine? Some antibiotics."

Hradich seemed perplexed. "But you have antibiotic". He gazed at Gwen and Frank. "You give to girls."

"What I gave to your girls is the wrong antibiotic for Nurse Pakin." Frank cast a glance at Richter, then to Hradich. *I gave them to more than just your girls.* "And our last supply truck had everything but *our* antibiotics. So we're almost out."

Richter's eyes rolled toward the ceiling. Hradich was looking at Frank.

"What is antibiotic you need? If I can fix, I do. You fix Zivka for me."

"Good," said Richter nodding, with a pleased inflection in his tone.

"I need two antibiotics," said Frank. "I need one called Cipro. I need sixty, five-hundred-milligram tablets. And I need Clindamycin, three-hundred-milligram capsules. One hundred and twenty of those."

Hradich looked bewildered again.

"I'll write it down for you." Frank got up and went to Richter's desk. He took a pen and a sheet of paper. "Okay, Colonel?"

Richter nodded.

Frank wrote them down. "I'll also write down the injectable version amounts we could use." He glanced toward Hradich. "In case one type or the other is available." He handed the list to Hradich. "Then there's the issue of how do we pay?"

Richter leaned back in the oak chair. "We cross that bridge when we come to it."

***

Hradich was back early the next morning like he had said he would be. He seemed determined when Frank first saw him in Richter's office.

The colonel started. "And what did you find?"

"I can get antibiotics," said Hradich. "I can get Cipro five hundred. Sixty tablets."

"Good," said Frank. "And…"

"I can get clinder, ah, clindu. Shit."

"You mean Clindamycin," said Frank.

158

"Ya," said Hradich. "One hundred twenty capsules Clindamyacin."

Frank quickly forgave the man. He went to Hradich and embraced him. Hradich stood there, arms limp. Frank then held him at arm's length, smiling broadly. Hradich managed to crack a smile too. But Frank caught the almost invisible quiver in the Bosnian's lips.

It was as if they had managed to come together in a common cause and set aside all the doubts and misgivings they had held about each other. "So this comes from Sarajevo?" said Frank.

"No." Hradich backed away. "Come from Banja Luka." He hesitated. "And…"

Frank and Richter both said, "And?" together.

"And. Need to pay."

Richter said, "How much."

"First. Need twenty-kilo sack of sugar."

What?

Richter looked puzzled. "Why do people from Banja Luka need a twenty kilo bag of sugar?"

"Is not people from Banja Luka," said Hradich.

"Then?" said Richter.

"Is people bring medicine to me *from* Banja Luka want sugar."

"And?"

"Number two. Cost of medicine."

Here we go.

"Five thousand American dollars. Cash."

Richter's eyebrows formed a chevron. "Five thousand American in cash?" he said loudly.

"That's a lot of money for that medicine." Frank thought the actual cost would be around fifteen hundred dollars. "Cash?"

"Is war," said Hradich. "You need. You pay. And ya, like you say in United States, cash is king."

Of course it was completely logical. Frank knew that. These guys weren't taking cheques or credit cards. But the price of the drugs. He knew Richter had a stash of cash somewhere. Every C.O. did, for situations just like this. It was in a safe somewhere or in a strong box under a floorboard. Usually around twenty thousand carefully accounted-for dollars. But would he give up five thousand for some antibiotics worth fifteen hundred, at most?

"That is all?" said Richter, looking like he was going into bargaining mode with the natives.

"No," Hradich said with his hands on his hips. "Doctor Frank comes with me to get the medicine."

"What?" Richter exploded out of his chair. Sending it crashing against the wall like a piece of debris launched in a hurricane, the chime from the spring in the chair going on. "I can't allow that.".

Frank waved his hands toward the floor. Trying to calm Richter down.

"Colonel," said Hradich. "What is matter?"

"I cannot let my surgeon leave my mission. That is against all rules." He thought it over. "And why do you need him to go?"

"Colonel. I am UN Liaison. Doctor Frank is *hero* for some of these people. They bring medicine and want sugar. And they want see doctor." Then he laid his ace on the table. "Need doctor to check medicine. Make sure right stuff. Make sure we not cheat."

Richter didn't have anything to counter that point, except a long stare.

"Colonel, I think we can manage this," said Frank. "He is the UN Liaison." He desperately wanted to buy into Hradich calling him *Doctor Frank*.

"Ya," said Hradich. "If he not safe with me, then with who?" He surveyed the room. "He fix my Zivka. Now I help. I fix."

The room fell silent. The tarpaulin covering the window was glowing so bright with the morning sun that the heat pearled beads of sweat on everyone in the room.

Finally Frank said, "Colonel, I'm prepared to take this minor risk. Sergeant Pakin needs to start the antibiotics, badly."

"Ya," said Hradich. "Is good."

Frank said to Hradich, "What about land mines in the roads?"

"Roads mined mainly north of Sarajevo. Not here."

Richter nodded.

That was all Frank needed. "When do we leave?"

A crocodile smile came over Hradich's face. "Leave eight in morning tomorrow. My truck."

Frank looked at Richter, standing a few inches taller than himself. And he thought about what must be going through his mind. All of a sudden, the Liaison is in control. But they had no alternative. No drugs. No access to them. No backup. Only cash.

The bigger issue was just coming into focus in Frank's mind: how could he understand Hradich's sudden change in attitude—both ways?

THIRTY-FOUR

They had gone to bed early. As much as Frank had wanted to make love to her, he couldn't. The thought of her ankle crept into the forefront of his mind again and again. Even though he held her tight and ran his hands over her thighs and abdomen, he couldn't. He pulled her face toward him, stroked her hair and kissed her. Felt her breath on his lips.

Gwen had rubbed him gingerly, as if her head was in the same place.

It was some time before they talked.

Gwen finally rolled on her side and propped her head on her hand. "I wish you weren't going."

"It'll be all right. But I know what you've been thinking. I've been there too. I've felt it. Just like you."

She cut him off. "I've been on relief missions before, so I've seen the mixed messages."

"Look, Gwen, everywhere I've gone, I've been ambivalent. You doubt this one. You doubt that one." He took her finger as it was approaching. "But Richter's right. This isn't like Africa, where you see thousands of people dying. One day it's Hutus and the next day it's Tutsis. Hradich is right too. Nobody has bothered us. And we haven't seen civilian casualties up here."

"Except for the rapes."

"Except for the rapes," said Frank. "And the empty villages."

"Well, Hradich still spooks me." Gwen shook her head. "The way he looked at you when he knew you were doing Babic's girls."

"That was some time ago. And maybe he's just a control freak... You know. See them all the time in the military."

"But what if he's picked sides?"

The room was silent and dark. Even though he couldn't see her clearly, he felt her attention weigh heavily on him, like a military pack on his shoulders. He knew she harboured her doubts, and there was little he could do about it.

Frank said, "All right then, what's the alternative? We sit here and wait for the situation to get better. For the roads or the airspace to open up while your wound festers, so someone official can bring the drugs up here?" His voice grew louder. "That's not acceptable."

Gwen didn't say anything.

"Hradich worked this out like he's supposed to. He's the UN's man. And I agree, he's not perfect. But he's the best alternative we have under the circumstances. Your leg can't wait any longer. So, I'm going with it."

She rolled over and pushed her buttocks up against his side. Frank turned toward her, and she pushed her buttocks into the cleft of his torso and legs. He put his arms around her and they were soon asleep.

***

In the morning, Frank met Richter in his office and received the fifty, one-hundred-dollar notes in an envelope. Five thousand American dollars—as specified. Richter also handed him a satellite phone and a paper with some numbers written on it.

"Just in case," Richter said. "Be careful. And make sure they're the right drugs." He patted Frank's shoulder. "I know you will."

Frank understood that was his main duty. And they all would have preferred the problem to have gone away. But that simply wasn't going

163

to happen. He also wondered where Richter's head was regarding the drug theft. It was as if that issue had simply gone away, vaporised.

Frank said, "I'll be back as soon as I can. This shouldn't take until 1800 hours. Besides, Hradich has the roads worked out. I've seen him drive from the back of my quarters."

Earlier, Frank had breakfast in the canteen with Gwen. And they had seen Father John. The priest had been visibly absent in the recent past.

Father said to him, "Go safely, my son. May the Lord watch over you."

"Thank you, Father."

But as he was leaving, Father John turned back and said, "You know, I can't help but think we wouldn't be in this predicament but for what you've done."

"Father," Frank had said, "the predicament was already here. All I did was respond to it, in a conscientious way."

Frank didn't like the disdain plastered on Father's face as he left. And he suspected John might have other issues—but he didn't have the time or the inclination to think about it.

The time had come for Hradich to arrive. Frank went to his quarters, changed into his regulation boots and put on his fatigues and military tunic. He put the envelope containing the money in the inside breast pocket. The phone was in his right pocket.

Frank had said goodbye to Gwen after breakfast. She had things to do in the clinic. Besides, he knew how ambivalent she was about the whole thing, wishing too that it would just go away. And perhaps a little pang of guilt, because this was after all, about her ankle.

He was determined. He would see this thing through with Hradich. He had navigated worse dilemmas. Frank smiled to himself.

***

Hradich arrived in his customary fashion, in a flurry and a cloud of dust. His pickup stopped in the square. He and another man with a submachine gun climbed out. There were two other armed men in the back of the truck.

Richter came out of the main building, looking surprised.

Richter said to Hradich as he crossed the square, "What's all this about?" He pointed to the other men, and by inference, their guns.

Hradich threw his hands up. "Is Yaro," referring to the man beside him. "Is insurance. You think I drive to Banja Luka in war, with doctor and five thousand dollars, with no insurance?"

It made perfect sense to Frank. *Why not to Richter?*

"You have cash?" said Hradich.

"Yes." Frank patted his breast pocket.

"And sugar." Hradich pivoted back and forth on his heels. "Need sugar."

Richter was almost at the canteen door. He opened it and called Dayna.

She came out with the bag of sugar across her left shoulder. Her big grin was present as usual, almost as wide as she was round. She walked over to the back of the grey pickup, as if she knew exactly what to do. Which, if Frank knew Richter, she would have been told. In detail.

One of the men in back of the truck took the sack from her and laid it carefully on the bed of the truck.

Dayna uttered, "Hmm," and started back to the canteen door without her smile.

Richter walked up to Hradich., "When do we expect you back?"

Hradich didn't miss a beat, "Six hours. Maybe seven. Eight hours, most."

"Good," said Richter. "I expect the doctor back here with the drugs by 1600 hours at the latest." He looked distinctly unhappy. "Otherwise…"

Frank thought he must have regretted saying *otherwise*. Because, really, what could he do? He was only betraying his insecurity.

"Very well," said Richter. He put his hands on his hips. "You can go."

Frank walked to the truck and noticed Richter following his progress. He saw Yaro, the man with the submachine gun, get in the back of the truck and pull up the tailgate. Hradich was in momentarily, beside Frank in the cab of the pickup. He wore a serious stare, which was somehow reassuring to Frank. The Liaison started the motor. As the truck started moving, Frank looked back to see Richter walking toward the main door with his head hung down. Looking past him to the clinic window, he saw the far corner of the tarp pulled up. Although he couldn't see her in the darkened room, he knew Gwen was watching him leave.

THIRTY-FIVE

Hradich drove down the hill behind the compound with speed and confidence. He wasn't swerving, as if he were trying to avoid anything. Like land mines.

At the bottom of the hill they were driving through a valley of browned grass with occasional patches of trees, mainly large oaks with curiously twisted trunks, the trees Yugoslavia was famous for, with their intricate grain patterns.

The dirt road meandered south through similar countryside for about five kilometres. There was no sign of civilization.

That had been the point of the relief mission, far enough away from any pocket of population that it would neither be associated with any particular side nor targeted by association in the event of a local skirmish. Typical UN policy.

Hradich turned east onto another dirt road, which he also drove with impunity.

Frank decided to break the silence. "It's such a beautiful country. Too bad there's a war."

"Ya." Hradich didn't take his eyes off the road.

"And there's no sign of any fighting here."

"Fighting mainly in south."

They were passing through a grove of spruce trees, tight up to the side of the road, obviously an unkempt area of wild growth. Straight ahead some buildings came into view. Momentarily they were in a village of mainly cinderblock buildings with A-frame wooden upper storeys. These were interspersed with traditional stone-foundation buildings with timber upper floors.

In the centre of the village they turned north onto a paved road, and passed what looked like a general store. A dark-haired man in the doorway watched them drive by. At the edge of the village was a hedge of cedars and a fence dividing off a farm. The house was set about three hundred metres off the road, an older stone building with smoke curling up from its chimney. A stone barn stood nearby with a thatched roof. Sheep fed in the fields and in a far corner a few Bosnian Mountain Horses grazed, all black, with a typical stature of only five feet.

They drove on up the curving road, crossing an arched stone bridge, which narrowed to one lane.

There were other farms, some with goats. Other fields planted from side to side with corn and wheat. Cedar hedges were common. Rolls of baled hay lay scattered in the fields. The practice had started in Europe in the eighties and had come to North America much later.

They drove in silence for about forty minutes. Frank figured they had gone north roughly forty kilometres, and would be somewhere around thirty kilometres north and five kilometers east of the relief mission. He remarked at how similar this place could be to the States, except for the infrastructure, the houses, and the short horses. He was actually enjoying the drive and the views, being out of the clinical setting—out of the pressure-cooker.

The topography suddenly became hilly. The road went up and down and wound through continuous stands of spruce trees intermingled with patches of oaks.

Frank knew from his briefings with Richter that the wooded hills were a loose demarcation line between the Bosnian Serb area to the south and the more Muslim-populated Herzegovina to the North.

Hradich said, "Is logging area from long ago. New trees plant."

They drove on for another fifteen minutes. Frank peered into the back of the truck at the three men. They eyed him back, dispassionately. One man gave a little wave with his free hand, the other cradling his weapon. The men were typical: dark hair, swarthy Mediterranean appearance. One with a peaked tweed cap. Wearing olive drab tunics that must have been from some military surplus store. Frank turned back to the front. He noticed Hradich looking straight ahead. He was surprised that Hradich had said anything at all.

The hills flattened out and the truck slowed. At the bottom of the last hill Hradich pulled onto a narrow dirt road, going into a tightly packed spruce forest. The branches scraped the sides of the truck. It was obviously an old logging road.

Frank said to him, "This isn't the way to Banja Luka."

Hradich turned to him and said, "Not going there. People Banja Luka meet here."

That made sense too. They were at least ninety kilometres from the city.

They came to a clearing of about a hundred and fifty metres across, with an old stone building that was obviously abandoned at its south side. There was a maturing spruce forest all around. The dirt road continued ahead.

Hradich stopped the truck.

Frank heard the tailgate drop. The men were talking in some dialect, and the lack of motion of the truck must have signalled them to jump out.

Hradich turned to Frank. "We go meet contacts Banja Luka." Then he said, "Leave phone. Make suspect."

Frank pulled the satellite phone out of his jacket and put it in the glove box, bending the antenna.

They got out of the truck, not bothering to lock it, and went to the back to join the men.

Two of the men had AK-47s, and Yaro had his Beretta submachine gun which he shouldered with a sling. The man with the cap threw the sack of sugar onto his shoulder. Hradich shouldered a rifle.

He said, "Let's go meet," and gestured toward the road on the other side of the clearing.

Just as they were starting out, there was a rustling from the field opposite the building, and they turned around.

Three young men, boys really, scrambled out of a depression in the ground. The tension from Hradich's men radiated like heat from an over-stuffed wood stove. The hand of the man with the peaked cap trembled on the sack of sugar.

Hradich squinted, like he was trying to understand.

The three short men came closer. They carried sidearms and measured their paces.

The leader was the middle one. Not five feet tall. Muscular. A cigarette in his mouth. The pack rolled into the sleeve of his white t-shirt. His head and eyebrows were shaved. He holstered a pearl-handled revolver on his right hip.

He said in a cordial Yugoslavian tone, "Where are you going?"

Hradich and his men remained motionless and said nothing.

Frank felt his heart pound.

The shaven one said again, "Where are you going?" His hand dropped to his holster.

Instantly, Yaro rotated the Beretta and loosed an automatic barrage before the boys' hands got to their guns. They fell to the ground, bleeding. Groping. Yaro walked over to them. The shaven one was going for his revolver. Yaro fired once into his skull. Blood splattered the ground under his head, and his eyes bulged out.

His motion stopped.

Yaro went to the next one, who wore a shocked expression. He fired once into his head. Then at the last boy's side he saw the Beretta's breech was open. He got a fresh magazine out of his pocket, inserted it, and closed the breech. He fired one shot into his skull.

Yaro turned to his comrades and waved them over with a nod of his head.

The one with the peaked cap put down the sack of sugar and went over with the third man. They dragged the boys back into the hollow in the ground from where they had emerged—what had likely been a root cellar. They left a bloody scraped path in the gravel, the last testament to their existence.

Hradich turned to Frank and said, "Robbers."

The surgeon stood there with his mouth open.

As if on cue, a buzzard and a crow landed in the treetops and cawed.

Hradich spoke as if he understood Frank's anguish. "They see sugar, they kill." He let it sink in. "When you dead, they take watch and teeth. You, they find bonus." He patted his breast pocket. His lips were quivering ever so slightly as he said, "You think?" Then he laughed.

Frank knew the country was full of these armed gangs of children. Happy that he wasn't dead, he thought of Africa. How people's fortunes suddenly changed. He inhaled deeply but didn't feel relief. He smelled the spent gunpowder.

Another buzzard arrived in a tree, looking at his predecessors on their perches and the prize on the ground. The pecking order was established.

Hradich said something to his men that Frank didn't understand. He turned to Frank and said, "You carry sugar. I need insurance." There was a pause. "We go."

***

Richter had been avoiding her. But he needed to know. Here they were now, out in the open. In front of his quarters. Walking beside each other, with no-one else around.

The colonel turned toward her and said, "Everything good with you?"

She turned toward him and said, "Yes."

He said, "Smile, at least."

She did, with a shoddy impression of nonchalance, that could be expected from a lesser rank.

"What did you get?"

"Eight hundred and eleven, American."

"That's all?" He wanted to turn and face her, but he didn't. "You know I've always made sure you came along."

"Of course. But eight hundred is what it was worth. We did the math. I grabbed the extra, as you would say, 'against his protestations.'" She looked at him for a moment. "The only other money in the box was funny currency."

Richter knew she delivered. And she had made the right call; other currencies would be hazardous in a problem situation. Better no temptation. But he had expected more.

Chief operative word—More.

He said to her after looking around, "You'll deliver my share before we leave. Keep the extra."

How generous. Eleven dollars or eleven hundred? Which was it really?

Jennifer turned and walked away with a certain swagger.

Colonel Richter wondered whom he could trust.

THIRTY-SIX

They were walking the dirt road, and Frank was labouring under the weight of the sack of sugar. Twenty kilos. Almost fifty pounds. He wasn't used to this. He was starting to sweat, swaying back and forth in the dips of the road. Falling behind. Hradich and his men were swaggering before him, like a group of men out on a Sunday walk after church.

The irregularity of the ground and the weight of the sack of sugar made his walk weary. Spruce branches on both sides intruded into his space.

That was when he noticed. And he chided himself for not seeing it before. He quickened his pace, sometimes almost stumbling forward. He confirmed it when he got close enough, looking at Hradich's back. He wasn't carrying an AK-47. He was carrying a sniper rifle. To Frank it looked like a Sako TRG.

Why would he have that? Not for fending off the locals. Where did he get it?

Frank had questions. But Yugoslavia was the most armed country on earth. He knew that. Apparently nine arms per person. So why not a Sako TRG?

But he kept falling behind and having to catch up. Hradich's men never turned back to check on him. They were having their own conversation.

At one point Frank realized that the sack was such a weight that his nostrils were flaring for air. He smelled the spruce trees. It reminded him of a Christmas long ago, when he was a boy. They had gone to Aspen, Colorado, and even though his father was located out of town—was it at Tall Meadows—they had gone into town. There was a park. Paepcke

Park. Frank had wandered in under the boughs of a giant spruce tree all decorated with coloured lights, and somehow he remembered the smell of that tree was just like the ones here.

The dirt road went on and on. Up and down. Mainly straight. The road and the sack of sugar were becoming such a burden...

He went on, then, swerving and tripping in a puddle of water, Frank fell to his knees.

That stopped Hradich. He looked back and said, "What's matter?"

Frank got up dirty and wet, but smiled. "The sack is heavy—when you carry it for a while."

"Ya." Hradich seemed unhappy. "Get go." He turned back around and resumed walking with his men.

Frank checked his pocket to make sure he hadn't lost the envelope. It was there. He followed the Liaison and his men. His walk was becoming more laboured on the uneven, abandoned logging road. The new growth spruce encroached ever closer and began to feel like it was closing in on him.

At one point Frank thought he might be left behind altogether. But there seemed to be a clearing coming up. He got glimpses through the trees. He noticed Hradich's group had stopped. They were standing at the edge of a farm field, watching him slowly coming up the road with a look of disdain on their faces.

They had formed a crescent at the edge of the field, and Hradich and one of the other men were having a cigarette. Frank walked into their midst. They threw their butts into a puddle.

"This it," said Hradich.

That made Frank quite happy, thinking it was the meeting place, not having to carry the heavy sack on the uneven road any farther.

He said, "We wait? We meet here?"

"No. Not wait."

Hradich's right hand went in under the back of his tunic. He pulled out a six-inch buck knife.

Frank wondered what he was going to do with it.

Curiously, the other three men were smiling at each other.

Hradich grabbed Frank by the collar, pulled him close and cut a deep crescent, the shape of a half moon, into his right cheek.

Frank yelled. He dropped the sack, put his hand on his cheek and probed the inside of his mouth with his tongue. *Didn't go through.* He was bleeding badly.

One of the men butted him hard in the solar plexus with his AK-47.

Frank sank to his knees in pain. He yelled, "What's that for?"

"What for?" Hradich grabbed the rifle and clubbed him once on each temple. "Is for you." He laughed.

Frank was seeing stars.

Hradich bent down, yelling at him. "You stupid American shit. You think you come here, cheat Kamenko Hradich?"

Frank could smell his breath. Feel droplets of saliva.

"No. You not cheat me." He butted Frank in the groin and pulled him back up again by his hair. "You come here, my country. With UN. You think you fix?" The butt got him on both sides of the jaw. Yelling, "You fix nothing!"

Frank was getting delirious. "Are you killing people too?"

Hradich stood up and stepped back and forth in front of Frank. "What matter?" He took his time. Looking around, he raised a hand, like he was considering a philosophical question. "In hundred years, what matter if enemy die now, or ten, twenty years? Not matter. Nobody remember." He developed a faint smile—a satisfied smile. "For me, better they die now. Make less trouble."

Hradich had a pistol in his right hand and a determined look on his face.

Frank was wondering what he should do. Was this the time to grovel? Plead for mercy? He was so bewildered and brow beaten.

Suddenly, Hradich's expression did a hundred and eighty degree turn, from one of anger to one of fear. He was looking around, crouching a bit. So were his men.

Frank thought he might have heard the sputter of an approaching engine. A truck engine? Then he couldn't hear it any more.

Hradich and his men were crouched, peering through the trees, for what to Frank seemed like an eternity.

He was kneeling in a puddle, swaying. His hands on his stomach.

Frank closed his eyes, enduring the pain, wondering how he had ended up here. Of course he knew. Barely in control of his faculties. There was a glimmer somewhere in the back of his mind. A glimmer that said, if only he had heeded his suspicions...

The sound of the truck was gone. *Must have veered off.*

Then he thought he heard movement.

He opened his eyes. The dark butt was approaching his face.

Frank's world went black.

THIRTY-SEVEN

He was cold. The headache. His stomach! His back was stiff, as if he had been laid out on a slab. Worst of all, he couldn't see.

Frank had no idea how long he had been lying there. It must have been a long time; he was so cold. He'd shiver if it didn't hurt so much. But there was no pain in his back. Or in his limbs. He wiggled his fingers. They were like icicles. His toes—not much better. He opened his eyes, and his world stayed black. His eyes ached.

He couldn't remember how he had gotten here. Or why. The surgeon in him said he had suffered a catastrophic injury. And a head injury.

Where am I?

He decided to take a deep breath. That hurt his head, his chest and his stomach.

Must be in a hospital. Can't hear anybody. He thought a moment. *They see me. Yeah, they see me. I just can't hear and can't see them.*

He was alone. Isolated in his body. Disconnected from the outside.

I'm a doctor, a surgeon. Why aren't they helping me?

In his mind he was crying. But his body didn't move. Then faintly, between his sobs, he heard something.

Don't cry. Listen!

It didn't make sense. No sense at all. He should be hearing hospital sounds. Instead, he thought he heard birds in the distance.

Must be really bad. Hallucinating. Where the fuck am I?

The birds got louder. He heard rustling? Like grass?

Jesus Christ!

So afraid! He knew he was Frank. He just didn't know how he had got to this. There were two crescents like the frames of a pair of glasses in front of him. Frank tried to concentrate on the edges, but as much as he tried, the swaying crescents moved with his gaze, and he couldn't see around them. Moving his eyes hurt so much. He noticed that the oblong crescents were becoming more circular and moving closer together. The edges were becoming sharper until they met and the edges were round and shiny, like metal. The brightness was taking on colour—kind of blue. The middle of the circles remained black.

The bright parts slowly gained detail. There was a sky blue colour, and slowly, clouds came into view. Then he realized he was actually staring down the large bores of a double-barrelled shotgun.

His heart was racing. He sighed and peed. And he wanted to yell.

At the far end of the gun was a bearded man with a dark complexion. Was he quivering? He seemed to be as scared as Frank.

Don't spook. Don't pull the trigger.

They looked at each other for some time.

The periphery of Frank's vision cleared more, and he thought it must be very early in the morning. How did he get here? How long had he been here?

He decided it needed to be done. He raised his left hand with great pain and said, "Help me." He waited.

The man did not move.

"Please, help me."

Slowly the shotgun wavered. The man turned it away from Frank's face and sized him up. He cradled the gun in his left arm and let the hammers down.

Frank was thinking at six inches his head would have all but disappeared.

Neither one of them seemed to know what to do.

Frank was unable to appreciate the man's confusion. He looked around and saw what had brought him here. There were crows and buzzards in the nearby trees. Hadn't he seen that somewhere recently?

Frank held both hands out and said, "Help me. Please, help me."

The man was still looking Frank over, with what the surgeon recognized as an expression of surprise or disbelief. What could be so bad to make him do that?

The bearded man, who wore a plaid jacket, walked away for a moment. When he came back he didn't have his shotgun. He bent down and put his left arm under Frank's neck, cradling him and getting him up.

Spasms of pain coursed through his body, and Frank wanted to say, *This isn't trauma protocol.* But he was given over to circumstances.

They worked their way to a derelict old pickup with a wooden box in back. He was inserted into the passenger side.

They drove slowly through the farm field. Every irregularity transmitted to Frank as a jolt of pain, some of them like lightning.

The bearded man kept a careful watch all around, as if the sputtering of the old truck's engine might attract unwanted interest.

They arrived at the back of a farmhouse. The man was helping Frank in when a woman appeared in the doorway.

She was slight and tall in a full-length grey dress, with a white shawl covering her ears and the back of her neck. Tresses of long dark hair fell from her temples down her front. She would be a beauty of Mid-East origin to Frank, except for the contempt and anger in her eyes.

She started on the man in the plaid jacket with vehemence.

There were words between them that Frank didn't understand, gladly. The man waved broadly with his left hand. There were more harsh words and more arguing before the tone softened. The anger abated to a point that sounded like understanding—even sympathy. All of it was lost on the wounded surgeon.

They passed inside, and the farmer placed Frank on a chesterfield. The surgeon was painfully nauseated, and passed out.

***

When he came to, it was because of the feeling of dampness on his face.

The woman seated in front of him had a bowl of water on a table beside her and was cleaning his face with a damp cloth. She smiled now, and kind lines showed around her dark eyes and the corners of her mouth.

Frank knew from the sting and smell of the water that it was salted. He was in good hands, even if he was hopelessly sore.

He let his eyes drift around the inside of the house. It was of modest construction typical for the area, with exposed timber beams and rough plaster walls, modest older furniture and a kitchen with a wood-burning stove and running water.

Then he saw her coming from the kitchen, a younger version of the woman tending to him, with a worried smile on her face. Perhaps sixteen years old, with a deep red kerchief tied around her head and trailing down her back., as if in preparation for physical exercise.

It clicked for him then. Frank had aborted her. She had been the pleasant one with the attentive father who wore the plaid jacket. The jacket that was so out of place with all the others. He scanned the room for him. He wasn't there, but now Frank knew who he was.

Of course, he wasn't dressed like the others. He was a farmer trying to make do.

That brought back a flood of memories. Gwen. She was injured. Richter. Forward Doctors International. The relief mission. The UN. Yugoslavia. Hradich. Fucking traitor Hradich, doing this to him. Because they were getting antibiotics for Gwen. Five thousand American. Cash.

He inhaled a few panicked breaths. Then he intentionally slowed in the hope it would settle him down. The woman startled when he sat up to find his jacket. It was on the back of the sofa where he now sat. He grabbed it. Checked it. The envelope was gone. His heart raced.

Shit. Fucking shit, Hradich!

The young girl was sitting in front of him, beside her mother, obviously sensing his discomfort. Both women had the same high cheekbones. The beautiful dark eyes that seemed somehow sad. Only the mother's were more lined at the edges. The arched brows, straight nose, and full lips. The similar tresses of dark hair showing undertones of brown.

Frank somehow felt better with the two of them there. He understood their concern for him. It was payback time.

The daughter held up a mirror she had brought over. The corners of her lips turned down as she stared him in the eyes.

Frank shifted to see his reflection. He choked at what he saw.

His forehead was bruised with skin splits. Eyes were black as a raccoon and puffed out, almost swollen shut. Narrow, bloody eye-whites. A deep crescent of a cut in his left cheek scabbed over. His cheeks and neck were swollen and bruised.

He had seen this sort of thing before many times. From the other side. But looking at himself…

He sighed and leaned back on the couch in disgust, uncertain whether it was caused by Hradich for getting him here. Or for himself, for not knowing better.

This was the first time he had ever come so close—and it was in Europe! Close enough for carrion birds to be sitting in the trees around him, waiting for his demise. It must have been the birds that attracted the girl's father, ensuring that one of his animals wasn't dead. He wasn't expecting to find the doctor who had helped his daughter, beaten within an inch of his life. So unexpected, the man had levelled his shotgun at

Frank, cocked and ready to fire, until he had worked it out and suspended *his* disbelief.

And Frank had left his satellite phone in the truck. At Hradich's urging.

The whole thing would be farcical if it wasn't so gullibly stupid.

***

The next day, they were sitting at dinner, four of them at the wooden table.

Frank wondering whether there was a son, but was afraid to ask. If there was one, they most likely had sent him away. No memorials were visible.

The family said their *du'a* personally and looked at Frank.

He said, "May Allah provide nourishment and safety for those who have rescued me and give me this food."

The family smiled. Moustaffa, the father, said, "Let us eat."

Frank enjoyed a spicy bean soup with *ćevapčići*, paprika lamb sausage and *petica* walnut bread.

Moustaffa turned to Frank at the end of the meal and said, "Tomorrow, find way get you back."

Mia, the daughter, squeezed her father's hand, and with an adoring smile cocked her head and said, "*Tata.*"

THIRTY-EIGHT

Colonel Richter surveyed the people assembled in his office; the duty sergeant standing, Father John on a green leather chair, looking distracted, the base lieutenant sitting on a wooden chair, while, Gwen Pakin occupied the other leather chair. The room was suffused with the early morning glow off the easterly tarpaulin.

The colonel thought to himself, *First the missing drugs.* If only he hadn't gone there, or could put that behind him. *Then the missing surgeon and the money. What else could go wrong? What could go right? He was going to face harsh criticism. Maybe court martial.* He cradled his head in his hands for a moment.

Richter looked up, thinking he had to keep up appearances and discharge his obligations. "It's been three days since they left. I have had no news." He turned to the duty sergeant. "You have heard…"

"Nothing, sir. No word from either Major Lambert or Liaison Hradich."

"And you have been following protocol?"

"Colonel. To the letter," said the duty sergeant. "When they weren't back at 1800 hours on Monday, we called the satellite phone hourly. There has been no answer. In fact, there has been no connection. It doesn't ring." He seemed to feel the weight of all the eyes on him. "And of course, we can't go out looking."

Richter wanted the facts out on the table. Everybody needed to hear them to let it sink in.

He said, "The only logical conclusion is that some catastrophe has befallen Lambert and Hradich. Perhaps a land mine took out their truck. That would explain the phone being dead." He thought for a moment.

"Or they have been taken by some faction. Perhaps some new militia we haven't heard about yet. But," Richter turned up his hands a moment and let them fall back onto his desk, "the Liaison should have ensured against that."

He looked at Gwen and wondered what she was thinking. Other than for her obvious feelings for Frank, would she hide something she knew? To what advantage? Unlikely.

"So, Sergeant Pakin." She quickly raised her eyes from the floor. "Do you have anything to add?"

"Colonel, if I knew anything—anything at all—you'd be the first to know."

"Of course." said Richter, satisfied with her response and thinking it sincere. The weight of the stolen drugs always on his mind—and perhaps on him. He went on, "Of course I have informed UNPROFOR of this situation. They are keeping all their channels open to see what they can learn about the disappearance. Making inquiries. But until now they have nothing to add. No news at all about Lambert or Hradich."

"And what about the roads?" said Gwen. "Are they still mined?"

"UNPROFOR reports they are."

"And flying?" she added.

"NATO has initiated Operation Deny Flight." Richter tapped the desktop with the fingers of his right hand. "This is to stop the Yugoslavian Air Force taking action against any side and deepening the calamity occurring on the ground. To that end, NATO fighters are flying sorties daily to intercept any Yugoslavian military aircraft. This has resulted in Bosnian forces targeting NATO aircraft with surface-to-air missiles. In fact, as I understand, several NATO aircraft have been fired upon. Consequently, the only aircraft flying in this airspace are NATO fighters capable of protecting themselves from SAMs."

"Exactly how do they do that?" Gwen cocked her head.

Richter smiled. "A little-known technology called HARM. It stands for high-speed anti-radar missile." He beamed. "They take out the radar from a hundred and fifty kilometres away. Before they even know what hit them." He waved his hand across the table and nodded. "Can't see them coming."

"That's all very well," said Father John, looking perturbed, if not judgemental. "But I still think the whole thing wouldn't be an issue," shaking his head quickly, "if we hadn't waded into this abortion thing."

Gwen shot back. "I don't want to hear any more of your shit—any more moralizing. Of what God might think of our actions." She was leaning way over the arm of her leather chair, addressing Father directly. "There were no other casualties of war. The rapes *were* the casualties of war."

Richter had his hands up, trying to contain her.

"What Frank Lambert and I did for these girls, these young women, was their due in any civilized country." She fought back a tear and then wiped it away.

Father John looked perplexed, and the colonel noted the tremor in his right hand.

Richter got up out of his creaky oak chair. "Please. Please." He wanted to say, *Children. Children.* But he caught himself. "Let us not forget that we want to know what happened to Frank Lambert and Kamenko Hradich. And preferably we want them back." He sat back down. Gwen and Father John seemed to have put their barbs away. He turned to the duty sergeant, who raised his eyebrows.

"Very well then," said Richter. "If you hear anything concerning these two, you will let me know. Not that I'm expecting anything. As for me, I will keep you informed."

***

Gwen was lying in bed later that night rubbing her sore ankle. Actually, she was in Frank's bed. That was where they usually spent the night. She had been there the previous two nights, somehow hoping, deluding herself that if she lay in his bed long enough, he would simply come through the door at some point, smile at her and slip under the sheets. He'd have some sort of an explanation for disappearing. He'd dispel her feelings about Hradich.

But now, lying here for the third night in a row, she was thinking that her hope was empty. Or misplaced. Ignored by some greater power. Likely the power of reality.

Gwen had dealt with that sort of thing before.

Like a bad dream, she remembered her time during the Russian Chechen war, helping the overwhelmed Russians deal with their casualties and the displaced Chechens. Her NGO had her partly in the operating room and partly in the immunization clinic.

That's where she had met Abraham, a wonderful Jewish man, an infectious disease specialist with a raucous laugh and a kind disposition. They had taken a shine to each other. She remembered the way he looked at her and how she felt when he did. The way they got close with light touches added to the words that spoke more of a coming intimacy. Not rushed—one of respect, patience and tenderness. The sort of thing that grew day by day.

Gwen was in.

Just when she knew the final step was coming, they were in the immunization tent, tending to the displaced. At the door, a Chechen fifty-calibre round found his head, taking it off and bathing the entire tent in his blood.

She went back to Baltimore after that, worked at the hospital that lent her to Forward Doctors International for eight weeks every two years, and never talked about it again. She never opened up to another man—until Frank.

Gwen first met Frank on the mission in Rwanda but didn't get close to him. He was such an enigma then, the hard-working surgeon looking after people around the clock when he was on. Drowning himself in booze at the hotels when he was off. She knew he was split from his wife, which might have explained the behaviour. Or his drinking explained the split. Even though he otherwise appeared as a benevolent soul, he was just too wild to consider.

That mission ended.

Then Gwen was totally surprised when Frank showed up at the Bosnian deployment. She remembered the exact look on his face in the hangar at Sarajevo airport. Happily, he was a changed man—the rough edges were off. He was kind, inventive and compassionate. She liked him instantly.

It was reciprocal. And they clicked.

They clicked in person. They clicked in the operating room, and they clicked in bed. How they clicked in bed!

Gwen felt like getting up. She knew Frank had some cigarettes on the shelf. She decided not to. Maybe she'd open some wine. Take some solace there. She thought about it. *Not without Frank.*

She lay there thinking it over. She had lost her husband years ago in a bitter divorce and Abraham to a damn bullet. Now that she had found Frank—the new Frank—he was gone too.

Gwen wanted to talk to him, to know he was okay. Work with him. Eat with him. Sleep with him. She wanted to have him rub her belly in bed, massage her breasts and scratch her back. Rub her until she was wet. She wanted to feel him inside.

Everything he had done, that had so filled the hollow place in her soul, she wanted back.

She wanted the whole thing back!

Finally, Gwen turned to the door in the dark room and knew he wasn't coming through there tonight. Likely not tomorrow either.

Hope, the last thing she had, was being robbed from her too. These awful wars in the name of religion and other ideologies were emptying her out.

Feeling like a hollow shell, she rolled away from the door, pulled the sheets close to her chest and cried herself to sleep.

THIRTY-NINE

Moustaffa had told him the night before that he had a plan. It was now just after breakfast. The plan was simple.

Moustaffa and Frank would take the truck and drive around the long way to the highway, likely the one Hradich had driven up. They would get to the southern area of heavy Muslim population, basically the southern border of Herzegovina. That would be the hilly area with the young growth spruce. There Frank would get under a tarp in the back, covered with a few tools to keep the thing in place. The farmer had put a thick cloth mattress on the bed of the truck to keep Frank comfortable. They would then drive down the highway to the village and up the hilly road to the relief mission. If everything went well.

For insurance, they both had CZ nine-millimetre automatics from the family cache.

The plan was that if Moustaffa used the Western word *doctor*, Frank was to get up and help shoot their way out of the situation. He had two spare clips.

Frank remembered that Yugoslavia was the most heavily armed country on the planet, with an average of nine weapons for every man, woman and child.

They were standing outside, Frank putting the CZ in one pocket of his jacket and the clips in the other.

Sajra, the mother, was there, showing a wary smile at first and then letting it mature into a glow of affection for Frank. Her shawl was far back, revealing a lot of black hair. Her dark eyes looked exotic when she smiled. They were set far apart and wrinkled with kindness. Her mouth beamed wide with pleasure. She was standing in front of Frank, taking a last gander at the wounds she had nursed.

Looking at me, and she can still smile.

He felt compelled to show his thanks, even though he wasn't familiar with the cultural norms of these people. He would just have to be a Westerner. He held Sajra around the shoulders, and pulling her near, hugged her and said, "Thank you."

She held him close and said something in the local dialect.

They parted, and both looked at Moustaffa.

He smiled and shrugged. Everything was good with him.

Then Frank went to Mia, who still had her deep burgundy kerchief tied high upon her head, like an athlete. Looking as beautiful as her mother, only younger.

Frank and Mia embraced and pulled apart.

Mia said, "Thank you for me, Doctor Frank. And good luck. My *tata* will take care of you now."

"I'm the one who needs to say thank you," said Frank.

The women then went to Moustaffa and hugged him.

The men got in the truck and drove off slowly.

Frank turned back and saw Sajra's smile dissolve into an expression of worry as she turned back to the farmhouse.

The chimney was still smoking from breakfast, the wisps curling up into the grey sky as if they wanted to join the clouds. There were patches of blue, signalling a risk of bright sun.

Frank wondered why he thought about it that way. *A risk of bright sun.* As if he had something to give up. Something to hide. Although he obviously did want to hide from Hradich and people like him.

The truck went onto a westbound road with Chinese paving, asphalt poured onto gravel. Rough at the edges. They drove on for fifteen minutes through fields of wheat, oats, cattle and goats. Some of the animals in the fields turned and followed the progress of the slow-moving truck.

Frank worried that the animals might have Hradich's eyes.

The pair didn't speak as they drove, pre-occupied by the task and its dangers.

At an intersection with a paved highway they turned left. South.

Frank felt the tension running through him. He reached into his pockets to feel the CZ and the clips. They were poor reassurance. He spotted Moustaffa seeing him checking, wondering what he was thinking. But neither of them said a word. The truck undulated on the road. After some time they came to a ridge where the road suddenly went up and spruce trees encroached upon them. The farmland was left behind. They passed the road where Frank thought Hradich had pulled in.

The farmer pulled the truck to the side and stopped. He turned to Frank and said in his broken English, "Border. Need to get in back."

Frank understood the gravity of the situation. They were leaving Herzegovina. He nodded agreement.

There was no traffic. They got out of the truck and pulled down the wooden tailgate. Frank got onto the bed.

He wanted to say something but didn't find the words. He patted his right pocket, the one with the gun in it.

Moustaffa nodded. He didn't speak either, as if talking now might be a jinx. He covered Frank with the tarp and placed the shovels and rakes strategically so the tarp would stay in place. He put up the tailgate.

Momentarily, they were under way, the truck undulating on the curves and dips.

Frank, under the tarp, was hoping he wouldn't cough or sneeze from the dust. He felt relief from his claustrophobia when the tarp glowed with sunlight. He lay there for a while, until the pressure from the ammunition clips in his pocket bothered him enough that he carefully turned onto his right side. He hoped that he hadn't disturbed the tarp. He didn't sense any flapping. That was just the way it was going to be.

The turns and the ups and downs stopped. Frank thought they must be in Bosnia. Now he was getting weary of the CZ pushing into his side, but he didn't move.

∗∗∗

Moustaffa was gaining confidence with the sparse traffic he had encountered, looking at the farmland and marvelling at how similar it was to his. Looking in the rear-view mirrors and checking on the tarp. It wasn't loose. He was feeling a sense of fulfilled duty, payback for his passenger.

He was approaching the village where he knew he would have to turn right. A Bosnian stronghold. No place to stop. No place to have a problem. That would likely be the place for him and his passenger to come to their end, even if they shot their way out. He had felt that way before, bringing the girls up for their operations.

The doctor had delivered. Now he would too.

A truck approached. A grey pickup. It wasn't going fast. The man in the passenger seat looked somehow familiar. He slowed down. The man had a beret on, and he stared at Moustaffa with a look that betrayed disgust. He was a craggy man, obviously unhappy. They were gone quickly. In his rear-view mirrors, Moustaffa checked the tarps again. This was the first time he had brought his truck here.

Moustaffa was wary and unhappy.

He got to the village, the prosperous one with stone under A-frame homes, where he had to make the right turn. There were people looking at him. People seated at roadside tables outside a small café. With demitasses of coffee and glasses of wine and liquor. Men with suspicious eyes.

He was thinking about his passenger and the fragility of their situation.

Once past the village, the road was close with spruce trees at the edges. The nearness of the new growth comforted him as it shielded them from easy view. He made another right turn onto a dirt road. Then it widened out, dust billowing out behind the truck. Finally, he could see his objective, the mission at the top of the hill. Soon he'd be able to get his friendly intruder out of his truck and get home.

The old truck strained against the steep pitch of the hill.

The closer he got, the better he felt.

He pulled into the square.

The duty sergeant came out to greet him.

Moustaffa got out of the cab and waved the officer with the blue helmet to the back of the vehicle. "Come, help."

They dropped the wooden tailgate and moved the tools off one side of the stirring tarp.

Pulling the tarp to one side, the sergeant looked aghast and said, "Oh my good God! Major Lambert, *sir*. Let me help you."

Frank slid off the mattress and out of the truck with a hand from both men. He smiled but wanted to cry. Cry with joy.

The sergeant shouted toward the main building, "Colonel. Colonel Richter. Come!"

Richter burst out the door. He strode across the square, never breaking his momentum. He got up in front of Frank, and it took him a moment to realize who it was, unaccustomed to the dark raccoon eyes and the bruised jaw that was starting to yellow. The swollen neck and the deeply cut cheek. His expression softened.

More people came out. Father John. Dayna. A nurse and some support staff.

Frank brushed off the dust from his clothes.

Richter said, "What happened to you? Where have you been?"

The gravity of Richter didn't immediately sink in to Frank. Then it did. The German was looking him over like he was a lost possession, tarnished by dirt and dampness, but found again.

"And moreover," said Richter, "what happened to Hradich?"

Frank thought he could wait for a better moment, but he couldn't. He said, "He did this to me." He paused.

Richter gave him a look full of pity.

The main door opened again, slowly. Gwen poked her head out and slowly stepped outside. She seemed in a trance. Then she ran for the damaged shadow that was Frank.

Frank saw her stride break as she favored her injured ankle.

"Oh my God," she said, pulling him close to her, in front of everybody. "I thought I'd lost you." She ran her hand up and down his back. Then, seeing his wounded face, her expression became aghast. She said, "Oh no."

Frank could imagine what she was thinking.

"Whatever happened to you?" she said. Examining every wound in clinical detail.

Frank said, "Hradich."

Gwen shook her head, her gaze still on his face. Her hands stroked up and down his back.

Moustaffa, taking this in, said, "I need go."

Richter screwed his eyes into a chevron. "You need to come back and make a formal statement."

Moustaffa nodded, raised his right arm and smiled triumphantly.

Frank dug into his pockets for the gun and clips.

The farmer, still smiling, held up his hand. "You keep. Maybe you need." He turned to Richter. "I come back." He got into his truck, started the ancient motor and drove slowly out of the compound. The engine coughed.

The group circled Frank, full of questions. They could all hear the truck working its way down the hill.

Momentarily, there was a startling pop, followed by a massive explosion.

The group ran to the edge of the hill to see what had happened.

At the very bottom of the hill, the truck was barely visible under a cloud of smoke, blown apart and burning. The debris was scattered hundreds of feet.

Frank was suddenly overcome by shock and remorse, feelings that he knew everybody around him shared.

They observed it for some time. No apparent movement. No remnant of a human form. Only a tangled metal frame.

Richter said, "Must have been an anti-tank weapon." He sighed. "No point in going down there."

The group wandered back toward the main building. They stopped at the corner.

Richter turned to Frank and gravely said, "Hradich did this to you?" He moved one step closer to Frank.

That very instant, the building wall shattered and sprayed out, right behind where Richter's head had been.

The sound of a distant gunshot echoed in.

Richter put his hand to the back of his head, cringing and brushing the stone chips off his scalp. Scanning the area quickly, he ducked down and shouted, "Inside! *Schnell.* Inside."

They ran for the heavy wooden door.

Father John was the last one in, pulling the door shut. A round crashed through the door. Father cried out, clutching his shoulder. His jacket was torn, and there was blood.

Gwen and the blonde nurse immediately tended to him.

Richter shouted, "Everybody away from the windows and doors. Stay down." They were safely down against the outer wall of the duty room, which was thick stone, impenetrable to a bullet but not to other weapons.

Richter said to Gwen, "How is he?"

The two nurses had Father John's shirt off.

Gwen said, "It's very superficial at the base of the neck."

Frank knew about Gwen and Abraham. Him getting his head blown off. He could imagine the chill running through her.

Richter said to the nurses, "The shots both came from the east. So, take him into the clinic and patch him up. You will be safe there. And stay away from the windows."

The camp order had remained that all windows were to be shuttered or tarpaulined, *at all times*. Frank realized the wisdom of Richter's order, which he would not allow to be disobeyed. The order of an experienced leader. One who cared for the people under his command.

Richter ordered the duty sergeant, "Everybody on Station Two."

That meant everybody take cover inside. And stay there.

The duty sergeant went into the clinic, and momentarily he could be heard shouting the order through open windows.

Richter and Frank sat beside each other, propped against the outside wall, opposite the duty desk where the radio was.

The colonel turned to him and said, "Give me a rundown."

"All right," said Frank. "We drove out with no trouble. Hradich was driving like he had nothing to fear." He quickly brought Richter up to speed with more of the details. He told Richter that Hradich wanted him to leave the satellite phone in the truck because, *it might raise suspicion.*

"And you went for it?"

"Hey." Frank held his hands out. "We all trusted him."

"And then?"

"We got ambushed by some kids with guns. But Hradich's men outdrew them. Dumped their bodies into an old root cellar."

There was a heavy impact upstairs.

They turned their heads up.

Then the clatter of light metal.

Richter shouted, "The fucker shot off our radio antenna." He surveyed the room with an incredulous expression. "I think he wants to come for us." He thought for a long moment and shouted, "Sergeant."

The duty sergeant came in from the clinic and kneeled on the floor. "Yes, sir."

Richter said, "Break out the guns."

The gun case was right beside Dayna, on the wall perpendicular to Frank. The sergeant pulled out six AR-15s and six Beretta pistols, along with multiple clips.

Frank noticed that Dayna was staring at him in disbelief with tears flowing down her cheeks.

Frank smiled at her and nodded slightly.

She turned away, sobbing.

Jennifer was beside Dayna on the floor, head on her knees, hands covering head, massaging her crew cut hair.

Richter said, "Go on."

The room suddenly became bright with the orange-brown glow from the tarpaulins. The cloud cover must have broken.

"We walked east on this road, through a spruce forest."

Richter said, "How do you know it was east?"

Frank shot back, "The sun. I'm a fuckin' boy scout. Okay?"

Richter chuckled.

Dayna watched them, obviously not getting it.

The sergeant did crack a smile.

Frank said, "That was when I noticed Hradich's gun." The colonel seemed like he was going to ask, but Frank said, "You know how he always carried that AK-47 around?" Richter nodded. "Well, he was carrying a Sako sniper rifle."

Richter's brows formed that chevron again with all the wrinkles around his eyes. "Really. Was it a .308 or a .338 Lapua Magnum?"

"Well, if it's Hradich shooting at us from other hilltops and taking stones out of the wall, I'm betting it's the big one," said Frank. "So think about it. If you hadn't stepped forward toward me out there, he would have taken your head off." He let it sink in. "The shot at John was obviously erratic. He's probably agitated. Otherwise, he would have got John. Which makes me think *he'd* be thinking about coming to get us."

"Ya," said Richter. "So his weapon has an effective range of one thousand metres, plus. Our guns are limited to a hundred and fifty metres." He was staring at the floor for a moment, deep in thought. "We need help." Then he turned to Frank. "Finish your story."

"They beat my head until I passed out but didn't finish the job. The next day Moustaffa shows up." He thought about it and looked at Richter. "It must have been the next day, because it was morning. He took me in, and his wife and daughter nursed me back."

"Really."

"Yeah. Now it turns out we aborted his daughter. And he brought her here himself. She was the one with the dark red kerchief." He waited a moment. "When I remembered to check, I found the money was gone. But it was gone in the field. And Moustaffa didn't know it was there.

Richter breathed a sigh of relief, quietly.

Frank said, "Then today he drove me back. Put me under some tarps in the back of his truck once we got to the border, just past the logging road. The rest you know." He thought a moment. "How will we let Moustaffa's family know? We must have their contact information in the medical records." He was overcome by a sense of grief and sadness for Mia and her mother, What would they think of him now?

Richter said, "First we deal with this situation."

John and the two nurses came back into the room.

The colonel said, "Father?"

"I'll be okay." He smiled as he sat down. "A deep scratch." He lapsed into inscrutability.

Gwen sat beside Frank and put her arm around his back. She kissed him on the temple and pulled him close. All the while rubbing her left ankle with her free hand.

Richter said, "So, we have a deplorable situation. The UN Liaison has turned traitor. Likely a Bosnian Serb operative all along. Tried to kill our surgeon and leave him in Herzegovina for the other side to take the blame. Took the money we were using to buy antibiotics. Killed the man who brought my surgeon back home and is now shooting at us. Only problem—we're out-gunned."

"That sums it up nicely," said Frank with a chuckle.

Gwen poked him in the ribs, and Frank winced.

She hissed, sucking her breath in. "Oh! I'm sorry," she said, bringing her hand to her mouth.

"Don't be sorry," said Frank. "Just don't do it again."

"Very well." Richter looked around the room. "I will report our situation to the United Nations Protective Force Headquarters. I will ask for air support and evacuation."

"What air support?" said Frank.

"The satellite phone," Richter said to the duty sergeant. When he had it, he turned to Frank. "The UN has started Operation Deny Flight. To keep the Yugoslavian Air Force on the ground. Fighters from Aviano fly sorties continuously." He clarified, "It started while you were away."

Richter was poking at the phone like there was something wrong. He turned to the duty Sergeant. "It doesn't work."

The sergeant said, "Try taking the battery out and putting it back in."

Richter did so. He looked up. "It still doesn't work." He did it again. The phone beeped. "Ah. Damned technology."

He dialled a number he obviously knew well. After a moment he said, "This is Colonel Kurt Richter of station Zebra One. I need to speak to General Martin. It is urgent."

Everybody in the room listened to the colonel recount the story to the general.

At the end he said, "Very well, sir. I await your call."

FORTY

At dusk, they had finally crossed over to the officers' quarters, having been locked in the duty room all day. F-15s had made passes all afternoon, coming from one direction, then another.

Frank knew all about the planes and their armaments. Their HARM missiles—AGM 88s. And the Vulcan Cannons, modern Gatling guns. Plus infrared vision. You had to be an idiot, a hero or insane, to stand in front of one of those fighters. And no rifle was bringing them down.

The planes had brought a sense of order and relief back to the mission. Food had been passed around, but Richter still insisted on the shutters and tarps, and on minimal, fast excursions outside. Potties were being used inside where needed.

There had been no more shots fired at the mission complex. The snipers likely knew about the planes' detection systems and weren't risking it.

On the way to his quarters Frank had noticed Gwen limping again, badly.

Gwen and Frank sat at the white table later that evening. The lamp with the bare bulb illuminated the far corner.

She said, "I thought I'd lost you. I was beside myself. I can't imagine what you went through." She pulled his hands close. "It was hard. I cried myself to sleep every night."

"Never mind." He said. "I'll be all right." He reached over and stroked her hair, reassuringly.

"But it might not have gone *this* well." She pulled him closer. "Hradich could have killed you."

"I think he thought that I was going to die. From the head wounds. The battering. Or maybe from hypothermia." He kissed her forehead. "Anyway, he didn't hit me hard enough. Now you'll just have to put up with me." He caught her hand before she got him in the ribs. "Not nice."

"I forgot." She sputtered and chuckled. "You know I wouldn't have delivered."

"Na-oh. When you don't get your way, you're a steamin' bitch with a mean right hook."

She laughed quietly but shook the table so much that Frank joined in.

Then Gwen propped herself up on her elbow and said, "You know, Frank, I've been thinking. Even before you disappeared."

He turned to her. "I think I know where you're going."

"Really? Then you tell me."

"You go first."

"All right," she said, shuffling around uncomfortably under the table. "Seriously. I've been thinking about this. But after what happened to you and having you back, it all came into focus in the duty room. Waiting for the sun to go down."

"Go on."

"You've been on other missions. Tried to help people like these. So have I." She shook her head slowly. "They're all the same. We can't save them." She paused and snorted a tear in her nose. "If the fighting here stops and the UN gets its way, and we patch a few people up—you know what's going to happen. Don't you?"

"Yeah."

"Five years or twenty, or fifty will go by, and they'll start it all over again." She reached for a tissue. "I was in Chechnya when the Russians were trying to straighten that out. It was impossible. There's so much hatred.. You can't fix it. Those people will be killing each other twenty years from now. Or thirty. And now there's talk of a Western coalition going into Afghanistan."

"Your point?"

"What makes any Western power think they can do better than the Russians? That area's all the same." She blew her nose. "I can tell you categorically I'm not going to Afghanistan."

"Me neither."

"But Frank. I'm getting tired of this shit. I'm tired of war. I'm tired of helping people who can't be helped. But most important, I'm tired of the people I love," she reached over and palmed his chest, "being hurt by these wars."

He said, "I'm there." He stroked her hair some more with his right hand. "These last few days really woke me up. So when this is over and we get out. If we get out, why don't we go back to the States?"

"Together?" She sat up.

"Yeah. I mean it."

"Frank, I think we could make it. I mean I think we'd still get along, *even* living outside of a war zone." She looked around the half dark room, like she was trying to find something. She found it. "Just think what the people we were helping did to you. We don't need this sort of shit."

The thought struck him. They could get along. Even living outside a war zone. *What have we become—and why?*

"I'm serious." He stared at her intently. "Will you come back to the States with me?" She chuckled a second. "We can set up shop somewhere. Nothing over the top. I'll go back to a civilized job." He let it sink in. "If Boston doesn't work for you, we can go anywhere. We'll both get jobs easily."

Gwen was listening intently but didn't say a thing.

"I'd be happy and proud if you came with me."

"I'm in two hundred percent. I'm just so happy to have you back. We're going to get out of here." She sounded defiant. "We're going to make it. We're going to make it out of here and we're going to make it back home. To hell with all these fucking bastards!"

That's my girl.

After they lay down and the light was out, she turned her back to him and pushed her buttocks into his lap. She took his hand and laid it against her stomach. Gwen bent her injured leg and rubbed her ankle with her free hand.

Frank said, "I saw you limping this afternoon. Also when I came back."

Gwen turned to him. "It's getting real sore. Much worse. I try to ignore it. What's the point?"

"I didn't manage to get the antibiotics."

"Never mind. It's not your fault." She turned back and tucked her behind into his lap.

They lay there, awake for the longest time, taking in the reality of his return. Thinking about the future before they fell asleep.

FORTY-ONE

The colonel watched the work progress. They were outside a village, the stone buildings barely visible across the planted field and rows of trees. Smoke curled up from one chimney into the overcast sky, as if it were liberating spirits into the heavens, to join the departed.

A loader moved dirt into a central spot in the field. The diesel engine sputtered. Men with guns supervised the work.

The colonel leaned against the track of an idle loader, smoking a cigarette. He hadn't seen any planes that day. A good sign.

He took a last drag and threw the butt away.

He was pleased with the morning's work. Success was a process. Each step took him closer to victory. One careful action after another. Seeing this progress gave him great satisfaction. He reached for his satchel, pulled out a thermos and poured himself a cup of coffee. He unwrapped a *kifle* and bit into it. The sweet butterhorn pastry was filled with walnuts. The colonel savoured his snack as he watched the men work.

The field looked untouched except for the fresh dirt in the middle. But that would soon grow over too. Cat tracks? Well, what field didn't have cat tracks? At least for a while?

But the bigger issue was his identity. He was resolute that his identity needed to be kept secret.

A breeze came up, and he watched the tree branches sway in the distance. The smoke from the lone chimney suddenly cut horizontal. This country of his was idyllic. He was in love with Yugoslavia. The farm country. The snow-capped mountains. The warm seashore with its quaint villages and sun-kissed sand. Best of all, the food.

Soon, all will be better.

He folded the tinfoil wrapper responsibly and placed it into the satchel with his thermos, as a man came running up to him.

"Colonel."

They spoke a Yugoslavian dialect.

"Ya."

The man wore a herringbone ivy cap. He adjusted the rifle sling on his shoulder. He said, "There is one still alive. See? In the southeast corner."

The craggy-faced colonel picked up the field glasses from the loader's track and scanned the corner of the field methodically. He saw the problem. A human leg was waving back and forth above the ground. A left leg. Nothing else protruding. He put the binocular back down.

The man with the cap said, "You want I dig up and shoot."

The colonel seemed disgusted. He said, "No. Save the bullet. Just put on more dirt. He will die soon enough."

"Yes, sir." The man ran back out into the field, waving to the operator of the loader.

The colonel watched as the instructions were given. He took up the binoculars again. The boy must have found a pocket of air and didn't realize that they were still there. He'd fix that. The loader piled on more dirt and drove over the spot, back and forth to pack the black soil down.

He was unhappy with this process. Burying the men. What he would have liked to do was what the Russians did in Poland with the Resistance, when they invaded in the sixties. They hanged the men on lampposts or power poles and let the women watch them die. The men with the nooses around their necks would either slowly choke to death, or if they were dropped a short distance, they would have a brief erection before they died. They would turn dark and start to stink. Then the townspeople could cut them down and bury them.

That's what he would have liked. But with the UN here, they couldn't do that. They had to bury them to keep the process hidden—more civilized.

He was disappointed, but he did his duty for his commander, to a fault.

Soon the work would be done. They would be able to go home. The loader was leaving the field.

Out of the woods on his right two men were approaching. Between them they held a struggling girl of maybe fourteen. She had a kerchief on.

"See what I found for you, Colonel," said the first one. "You want her?"

A crocodile smile came over the colonel's face. "Ya. Up here." He motioned to the cat track.

The girl started to scream wildly. Squirming. Struggling.

The colonel stared into her face until he got her attention. He put his hand to his ear and turned from side to side, as if he was looking around for people who could hear her. Like a mimic in a show, he parted his hands in a quizzical gesture and smiled.

The girl seemed overcome by horror. She screamed hysterically.

The colonel felt the excitement like a tingle, and he started to get hard.

The men tore off her skirt and underwear.

The colonel was getting harder.

The girl screamed, and the first man struck her across the face. She quieted somewhat.

They hoisted her up onto the cat track, pinned her down and spread her legs open.

She started screaming again and took two more heavy hits.

The colonel loosened his pants, dropping them down, showing his full erection.

He quickly spent himself inside of her. She seemed to know it was over, because she stopped struggling. He pulled out and looked at his penis and her vagina. They were covered in blood.

The girl began sobbing.

The colonel saw the blood dripping from his penis onto his clothes. He said, "You pig. See this? You bloodied my pants!"

The colonel wiped the blood off himself with a napkin from his satchel. When he was done, he pulled up his pants and lit a cigarette. He gave one to each of his men and lit theirs for them.

They talked about the day's progress.

When the girl finally stirred, they turned to her and smiled.

The colonel said to them, "You want some?" He pointed at the girl, whose face was taking on a panicked expression again.

They both shook their heads.

The colonel shooed her away with a gesture. He said, "Go." When she didn't move, he shouted, "Run."

She reacted to the voice, shifted, and fell off the track.

The men didn't do anything but watch her.

She scooped up the remains of her clothes and standing up, covered her bottom.

The colonel malevolently pointed at her, and said, "Go. Go away."

She started to run to the far edge of the field.

The first man took his rifle and shouldered it. He said, "You want me to shoot?"

The colonel said, "No. A good girl. Let her go."

The man turned his rifle down. He said, "You happy, Colonel?"

"Ya."

The girl stopped. Looking back she picked up a stone and threw it at them.

The colonel felt a pang of anger but held his hand out so the men would not shoot.

They said a few more words as the girl disappeared behind some trees, running toward the empty village.

The two men got into the idle loader, started it, and drove off after the other one.

The colonel had his satchel. He picked up his Sako sniper rifle from where it was propped against a tree.

He was *so* happy with the day. There had been no planes. Colonel Hradich thought of one more thing he could do, maybe in the morning.

FORTY-TWO

Dayna was pacing back and forth. She had been consumed by this for hours. Not like it was a new thought, because she had figured it out days ago. Only she didn't want to react too quickly, didn't want to jump the gun. She had to get her head around all the possibilities.

An evacuation had to be coming. And if not, well, she had to out it. *And I will.*

She wasn't sure at first, how she'd broach the topic. Dayna looked around the room.

It was large enough, but at the same time it was dingy. It had an odour to it. A damp odour that Dayna put down to the age of the place, and maybe to Jennifer.

They shared it.

Two twin beds. A small white table with chairs. A few lamps with bare bulbs. And a Mediterranean armoir. There was a sink under the shuttered window with some cupboards on either side, and a bathroom.

How did the NGO's come up with this sort of shit anyways? She knew most of the rooms were similar. Oh well, not her doing, and not her problem for much longer.

Jennifer came out of the bathroom, past the cook.

That raised Dayna's blood pressure to boiling. She grabbed Jennifer by the arm and spun her around, face to face.

"Hey," she shouted, "what's that for?"

Dayna jabbed her in the chest so hard she hit the wall behind her, shaking the cupboards.

"You bruised my tit I'm going to report you. . ."

"Shut up you cheap bitch." She grabbed the white girl by the chin, pinning her to the wall. "You gotta know that title's too good for you. You're a thief, stealing from your own people. Yeah, I got a few things of my own I'm gonna report."

Dayna was not only round, but she was tall enough that Jennifer couldn't kick her while she was pinned there.

Dayna had her hand in her pocket and dug out a small round object. She let Jennifer go and held it up.

Jennifer circled the edge of the room like a caged animal, soothing her chin with her right hand. Watching, to make sure she was far enough away from the enraged black woman.

"So bitch, what do you think this is?" Dayna held up the pill.

They moved around each other like two fighters in the ring.

"How should I know?" Jennifer's hand left her chin and she went for the pocket of her khaki pants. She pulled it out with a look of disappointment.

"Well let me see, it's stamped Oxycocet 5." Dayna held the pill out toward Jennifer, and said, "Know what that is?"

Jennifer shook her head as she rubbed her left breast.

"It's a damn narcotic. Now, how did a fucking narcotic get into our room?"

"Where was it?"

Dayna waved it around in front of her, "It was caught in the grooves of the floor door." She bobbed her head from side to side. "You know—the one you go in and out of secretly at night. Before and after you go out. When you think, I'm sleeping." Dayna had her other hand up like she was going to club Jennifer.

"It could have come in stuck to our shoes," the younger woman screamed.

"Honey," Dayna pushed Jennifer right into the wall, and said, "Neither one of us goes into the clinic."

Jennifer's face was at the height of Dayna's breasts. The cook had Jennifer's arms pinned and was forcing the assistant's face down into the cleavage in Dayna's tee-shirt.

"You think you got one bruised tit? Well you just smother between these, because my black boobs are so big you can hang key chains from my nipples." Dayna was shouting. "And you're going to wish you *had* been smothered when I take this up with the colonel."

***

They had been up for hours.

Gwen got off to a bad start. Her ankle was very sore now and exuded a large pocket of puss. By noon Frank had examined it and decided that she needed to walk with crutches. There were no appropriate antibiotics in the stores.

Frank ventured across the square to speak to Richter, not even thinking about snipers and planes.

Richter said, "I spoke with General Martin yesterday. He is working on it."

Frank told him that Gwen's infection was getting worse. That she needed help, big-time. She needed antibiotics, or she might lose her foot or her leg. He was surprised at how quickly it had advanced.

Richter reassured him. He'd speak to General Martin again and let him know about Gwen's urgent problem.

Frank walked across the square back to his quarters. He warmed a cloth and put it on Gwen's ankle. He changed it every fifteen minutes and was amazed at how much puss it drew out. All from a tiny pore.

He spent the morning this way. Then the early afternoon. More hot cloths and more puss from the ankle.

The morning had come and gone. So had the afternoon, one hot compress after another. One door opening after another. He heard them all. Obviously, people were moving around. But Frank was staying with Gwen.

There was a break from the noise of the doors. A long break. Then one opened and closed.

Frank thought it was from the canteen.

There was a clatter of dishes outside and a thud. Moments later, a shot echoed.

Frank went to the door and cracked it open. He peered outside.

Dayna was lying in the middle of the square, shot through the chest, still writhing as she irrigated the hungry earth with her blood. The red patch flooded out to the dishes she had dropped around her.

Frank couldn't go to her, or he'd be next. Besides, there was really nothing he could do other than comfort her. Not with that massive hole through her chest. Her nervous system so shocked, she was likely unconscious. Feeling like he might vomit, he retreated into his room and leaned against the door frame, pulling in deep breaths.

Gwen turned to him and said, "What's wrong?"

Frank took some time. He sighed and softly said, "Nothing we can do." The deep breathing helped him. But he didn't want to tell Gwen. He didn't know why.

He mustered the nerve to open the door again. Dayna was there in the square, lifeless, taken out by a sniper. Across the square at the bottom of the main office's door barely cracked open was Richter. The duty sergeant was visible just above and behind him.

What none of them noticed, was the crack in the door to Dayna and Jennifer's room.

✳✳✳

Jennifer was lying on the floor looking out a one inch crack in the door. She was hyperventilating with relief. Sweating, after no exertion, she rolled onto her back and wrapped her arms around herself.

She knew it was going to be all right now, with Dayna dead. Even though Richter was on her side, they wouldn't have had to deal with a complaint. Out in the open.

What great luck the sniper took the bitch out!

She didn't have to do it and come up with some story.

Jennifer exhaled, slowed her breath and put the safety back on her Glock 9 millimeter. The one from special services that went through with her baggage.

She stealthily pushed her door closed, careful not to make a sound, still looking out, lying on her back.

Dayna lying there lifeless, soaking the ground red.

One less thing for her to worry about.

∗∗∗

Colonel Richter looked on in shocked disbelief. He nodded to Frank and shouted across the square, "I'm calling Sarajevo to insist on evacuation."

Sure, sure, thought Frank, leaning against the door frame, his eyes on the lifeless body in the middle of the square. He was overcome with a consummate emptiness, from the middle of his chest to the pit of his stomach. *Sure, sure. Just too late for Dayna.*

He turned to see Gwen sitting on the bed, staring at him. He felt some solace knowing they were still together and alive.

She said, "Frank. Are you all right?"

He looked back at Dayna again. He was ready to tell Gwen now.

Frank closed the door on the late afternoon sun. The inviting golden rays were inaccessible to those captives still alive in the relief camp.

FORTY-THREE

The day was not unusual at Ramstein. Just one thing…

A nice fall day. Bright clear sky with only the odd stratus cloud. Crisp air just before noon. Fall colours showing in the distant hills. Just one thing didn't fit.

Base activities looked normal with service vehicles running up and down the sides of the airstrips between the hardened bunkers sheltering the planes and the main set of drab green buildings. The large American flag was flying at full mast on the other side of the buildings. The solemn control tower and revolving radar arrays on the far side of the main runway. A group of F-16s was parked near the service hanger alongside some Black Hawk helicopters. Even a taxiing F-15, with all the noise that makes, was not unusual.

What didn't fit was a group of five helicopters close to the north end of the administrative compound.

They were all different. Foreign soldiers guarded the aircraft and chatted amicably with American servicemen keeping them company. All of them were heavily armed. The insignia on the planes were English, French, German, Italian and *Russian*.

General Carter stood leaning on both hands against the end of the conference table and said, "I'm very grateful, gentlemen, that we're in agreement. I must tell you that I have been authorized by the President of The United States to extract these individuals, with or without United Nations approval. Am I correct in assuming that you have all been given similar clearance?"

British General, Ted Fellows, said without standing, "Yes, Vern. I spoke with everyone here last night. We're fully cleared to go ahead with the mission with the one caveat, which is that we not be aggressors. This is, after all, a rescue mission by what amounts to non-UN-sanctioned forces acting quite independently. I must say that I'm quite delighted in this show of solidarity," and rubbed his hands vigorously, "but especially so with the participation of General Gogol on behalf of Russia." General Fellows, a burly man in camouflage fatigues with crew-cut red hair, smiled, looked at General Carter and turned back to General Gogol. "I only hope that we can pass on our traditional formality and speak as friends."

General Gogol, who was sitting opposite General Carter at the far end of the conference table, spread his arms out wide and said, "Call me Yuri." He laughed, so raucous, deep and infectious, the whole table joined in.

That might raise the eyebrows of outside guards who were within earshot. The two dress-uniformed guards on either side of the outside door, however, did not flinch.

"I can't tell you, Yuri," said General Carter, "what a remarkable show of solidarity this will be to the UN, with you on board, and especially what this means to me. Personally."

General Gogol was wearing his grey dress uniform. His hat lay beside his left hand. He raised and lowered his bushy black eyebrows. "It will show them we are all on the same page," he said in a heavy accent.

There was approval from around the table and some amazement at his ease with the idiom.

"Now. My plan is very simple, gentlemen, if I can have your attention." General Carter turned and used a pointer on a large wall map of Europe. "Simply put, we're going to fake an air attack by US forces from the Adriatic Sea," he pointed to the coast of Yugoslavia, "while our helicopters come in from behind," he traced a path from southern Germany, across Switzerland and northeast Italy, "and evacuate our people of interest. The return will be by a slightly different route through

Yugoslavia to maintain the element of surprise." He panned his audience, looking for signs of disapproval. There were none. "Now, my suggestion to keep things simple is that we use American forces already in the Mediterranean to fake the attack." He turned to his aid, Colonel Davis, a tall lanky man. "What do we have in the Adriatic, Paul?"

Davis pulled some paper sheaves out of his valise, looked at them, and shuffled them before reporting, "We have the USS *Theodore Roosevelt* presently engaged in Operation Deny Flight over Bosnia-Herzegovina. That's their UN assignment." He looked up. "Sorry, sir. I'm not fully up on navy assignments."

General Carter turned, put his hands on his hips and stared at Davis unhappily. "That's what I thought. So what tactical group is on Big Stick?"

"That would be," more shuffling paper, "the VA/37. The Ragin' Bulls."

"Well! That's good news!" He wondered for a moment about Davis, but he knew those personnel and planes could deliver. He turned back to his audience. "Now. The VA/37 flies F-18 As, correct?" He paused and turned to Davis.

"Yes, sir!" He put his papers back in his valise.

"Right. One very fine interdiction aircraft. Turns out the navy's going to have an exercise." He beamed and raised his eyebrows twice. "The plan is to put an AWACS over that part of the Adriatic in the early morning. Not too much warning—just like a real attack. Fly by a couple of C-130 gunships. Scramble the F-18s at 0800 hours, fully loaded, eight of 'em. Have them group up over the Adriatic. There, they join up with Fighter Squadron 494 from Aviano. F-15 Strike Eagles. All twenty-four of them. Put up some helicopters and float some rescue boats. 0800 hours is late for an attack, but with the confusion in UN communications, when those planes fly low and fast toward the

Yugoslavian coast, I guarantee you every single piece of Milošević's radar is going to be pointing south."

There were smiles around the table.

General Fellowes said, "Like a wall of death, heading right at them." He panned the table. "Must say I'd give my eye teeth to smell Milošević's pants when he sees them coming."

More laughter.

"The only way Charlie will know our choppers are coming in the back door, is if they actually fly past a Serb installation." Carter paused. "For the navy and the air force, this is officially classed as a training exercise. We will be the only responsible operatives. And our governments, all seven, will take the flack at Security Council in New York next week." General Carter surveyed his audience. "Ain't that wonderful?"

Big smiles. General Gogol and Italian General Riccio were chuckling. Riccio, so hard that his coffee cup clattered on its saucer.

"As you know," said General Doyle, the tall Canadian, "the leader of UNPROFOR Yugoslavia, is my colleague General Larry Martin. I think we need to inform him, encoded of course, of what we're doing. I know him well——he'll go along with us."

"And that's in the plan!" said Carter, animated. "We're going to wait till the final hour. Just enough time for him to issue a notice to his forces, but not long enough to breach security. Also, bar civilian flights."

"Good. That takes me to my next point," said Doyle. "Regretfully, I have no rotary wing aircraft in this theatre. But my government insists on being part of the plan, especially the politics." He hesitated. "May I suggest we're hitching a ride."

"Come fly with us!" said Gogol, boisterous. Spreading his arms out. "Russian helicopters are big, and we're both from the north. We will make good company." He laughed deeply.

The German general, a stout square man, said, "We can always accommodate one."

"Our 'elis are small. Crew of *deux*. *Pardon*, if we shall pick up, how many? Twenty-two?" The French general turned to Carter as he twirled his black handle-bar moustache with his left hand.

"Yes. Twenty-two. One a woman on a stretcher. And one in a body bag."

"Then the French helicopter *est occupé*?"

"Don't forget, the Italian helicopter has much room too. It's Russian." Riccio and Gogol chortled again. "Canadians are always welcome with us."

Carter was beginning to wonder if Gogol and Riccio were spending too much time together.

Doyle looked at Carter, shrugged and said, "I guess we'll fly with the Russians." He turned to Gogol. "I'll send you two of my best. Fully armed, of course."

"I would expect no less. I'll tell my crew." He waved his index finger, "You will see how well they get along."

Ted Fellows spoke to Carter. He started slowly. "Can you tell us how your man got into such a fix?"

General Carter put his hands in his pockets and turned his gaze downward. He paced in front of the wall map for a moment and then looked at it closely. He finally addressed the other Generals. "It's a long story. Won't be long until the world finds out the biggest European genocide since the Nazis is going on right under our noses. The UN, of course, will do nothing."

Carter knew he had to level with them and tell them the whole story. "Frank Lambert is an American surgeon stationed at an advanced Forward Doctors International outpost, under UN protection. Now, Lambert wasn't getting any civilian casualties, but a local Liaison asked him to intervene with his raped daughter. The guy's a Bosnian Serb.

Fully cleared by the UN!" He let it sink in. "Lambert aborts her and the next thing you know, there are all kinds of raped girls—mostly without brothers! You know what that means! Anyway, that's all okay until he starts doing the same for the other side. So the Bosnian Serb Liaison figures, God and technology are on his side—and can't figure out why Lambert's people are betraying him—starts shooting at the outpost. There's one death from that. In addition, satellite imaging and intelligence points to the fact that medium scale field weapons as well as SAMs have been moved into the area. A showdown is coming. Hence, our problem."

"Yes, but aren't there some other factors?" said Fellows. "I mean, wouldn't we normally leave them there for the UN to collect? They're adults with guns. Surely they can protect themselves from a few Bosnian Serbs until the cavalry comes?"

"Well, it's a bit deeper," said Carter as he held up his hands. "There's no indication that UN sanctioned forces can get in there, given the unrest in Sarajevo and the local armament buildup around the mission. Plus an American nurse who's injured, needs evacuation, and can't wait. Also, I have to admit that Frank Lambert is my godchild."

Every eye in the room turned and was stuck on him.

"Let me explain." Carter swallowed hard. "Frank Lambert is ex US Air Force. I flew with his father in Vietnam and other theatres. He was one of the best pilots we had. He died in a VX gas accident at our facility in Utah. I always felt responsible, and I've been looking out for Frank ever since. That's the whole story."

The room fell silent for almost thirty seconds. Thirty long seconds.

General Fellows finally said, "Well. We shall just have to pick them up then, shan't we?"

"*Da*," said Gogol. He reflected a moment. "It is sad, I think, that the only people hurt by these ridiculous weapons of war are our own service men and women." A chorus of nods around the table.

FORTY-FOUR

The little boy followed the man into the emergency room.

The man said, "Help me. Help me—I'm dying."

The boy watched intently as the man, who was not very old, was draped over the shoulders of a young doctor and a nurse. They walked him in between them. A bewildering flurry of activity followed them to a stretcher in the empty treatment room.

"You've got to help me!" The man was clutching his chest as he looked up toward the ceiling. He was breathing heavily.

He is very sick.

"You're all right, sir. Relax. Sit back." The nurse in the white uniform helped him recline onto the head of a half-raised gurney.

The young doctor asked, "Do you have chest pain?"

"No!" The delirious man was swaying to sit up. "Can't you see I'm dying!" he insisted, clawing at his chest.

Can't they see how sick he is?

"Sir, try to relax." The young doctor pushed him back down onto the stretcher. "Monitor leads. IV D-5-W stat! Cardiac pack stat."

Another woman in a white uniform, a nurse, fumbled with his arm. "I don't see any veins!"

The little boy knew what doctors and nurses were. He had come here to get stitches.

An older doctor, they called him Doctor Prosser, came in. "What's going on?"

Another doctor came in. He was tall and had dark hair. He seemed kind. He moved closer.

Do I know him? The little boy tried to recall. *I think so.*

The young doctor said, "Came in off the street. No history. Says he's dying. Clutching his chest. That's it!"

A woman in a dress entered the room and said, "Medical records negative," and left.

"B.P. 60 over 22," said another nurse. "Pulse 160."

"Get an IV in!" The older doctor shouted. He put his hearing thing to the man's chest.

"Help me! Help me!" Squirming.

"Hold still please, sir." The older doctor, Prosser, put his hand on the man's chest.

"You're choking me. You're choking me."

Please don't hurt him. Please don't hurt him! He's my daddy. The little boy backed into the counter opposite the foot of the gurney.

"I can't get an IV in."

"O2 sats sixty percent."

"O2 one hundred percent mask." The older doctor turned to the tall dark-haired doctor, and said, "Frank, I need you."

Frank is my name too. The little boy's mouth gaped open.

The tall dark man went to the head of the bed. He was looking at his daddy's neck. He said, "Number twelve IV catheter." He threw some liquid onto his daddy's neck.

The boy could smell it right away. The liquid smelled like his daddy's breath after a party.

A nurse handed Frank a small plastic thing and steadied daddy's head, exposing the right side of his neck.

"Don't choke me. Don't choke me." Crying, and then, "Help me!"

"Monitor shows flat complexes. Rate one-seventy."

The tall man pushed the plastic thing into daddy's neck. He seemed unhappy. Angry.

Why is he angry at my daddy? He's just sick.

The tall man threw the plastic thing into a silver basin, and said, "Another number twelve."

"Help me." Daddy whimpered.

The nurse handed Doctor Frank the catheter, and steadied the man's head.

"Help me. You're choking me!"

The tall man seemed upset. Like he jumped a little bit. He pushed the plastic thing into the patient's neck, slowly.

Daddy cried out.

The nurse steadied his head.

The tall doctor pushed the thing in further.

The little boy saw a bead of dark blue blood coming out of the end of the plastic thing. *My blood is red.*

The tall doctor said, "I've got it!" He attached a plastic tube with a bag on it.

Daddy became silent.

Doctor Prosser was shouting for things.

Frank looked up and saw the little boy. He pointed at the child, like he was unhappy. Frank said, "Who is that?"

The young intern who had helped the patient in, said, "Walked in behind the patient."

Frank shouted, "Get him out of here."

The patient had his arm up. He mouthed, "Help me. I'm dying."

"ECG's flat."

"Shock him, 300," said Prosser.

The machine beeped ready.

A nurse applied the paddles and delivered the shock. Nothing.

"ECG's still flat."

"Do 300 again. Quick, two amps of bicarb."

The machine signalled ready. Then—whack!

Nothing changed.

Doctor Prosser, said, "Has to be tamponade." He turned to Frank. "Open him up."

Frank approached the table from the right. He spilled pink stinky liquid all over the chest and abdomen. A nurse helped him put on a green gown and what looked like rubber gloves.

Frank looked very upset.

The little boy was breathing fast.

A nurse threw open a green tray—Frank took a knife. The nurse stopped pushing on daddy's chest. Frank made a large deep cut across the abdomen, under the ribs.

Why are they cutting daddy? He shuffled his feet.

Frank didn't look happy. He said, "There's no bleeding." He put one hand into daddy's belly and took a long silver thing in his other hand and opened and closed it, like scissors. Grey-blue blood welled up and over the sides of the body, spilling onto the floor. Doctor Frank's feet were soaked with it.

"Complete asystole. I'm massaging him."

"Pour in the fluid," said Prosser.

***

Frank looked past Prosser, past the patient's feet and saw him again—the little boy. Standing there with his mouth open. Looking surreal. The teddy dangling from his right hand. The little boy looked up, pupils dilated, as if he was becoming some kind of an apparition. Like the Edvard Munch painting, The Scream—Frank felt he was looking back at himself.

Frank's heart pounded—stopped—and pounded, and choked him. He clutched his chest, smearing himself with blood. His chest was heaving. He tore at his chest.

The little boy was becoming more menacing. His eyes disappeared, becoming two black holes into an empty skull.

He had seen that before—in Africa.

Frank knew now! *I'm the little boy with the teddy.*

He turned to the patient. *My father.* Abhorrent, *No…* Like an echo.

Back to the little boy, his mouth open, an empty jagged hole.

It was killing him! *It was literally killing him.*

Prosser was taking it in—coming to Frank—reaching for him. His voice was fading, fading away.

He felt the rubbing on his chest.

"Frank. Frank." A woman.

He was waking up.

He felt the hand on his chest, tugging. He couldn't breathe; then he could.

"Frank. Frank. Wake up."

He knew it was Gwen. And, he remembered the whole thing. Just as suddenly, in the dark, he started to remember more dreams.

He saw Gwen, barely visible in the bed beside him. "I'm awake, Gwen." He wasn't sure his words were comforting her. He shifted closer to her. "I remember the whole thing."

"Sure you do."

They fell silent for some time. Neither one knowing what to expect. Or what to do.

Frank finally said, "I was a little boy with my father when he died." He paused. "And I was *me,* operating on him when he died. Like I was split into two different people."

She stroked his heaving chest.

Frank was not doing well.

"I'd completely forgotten that I was there when he died." He started to sob. "How could I…"

"It's okay," she said as she cradled him and stroked his hair. "It's okay." She held him closer. "We're going to get you some help."

FORTY-FIVE

It was one of those fall mornings, sufficiently far from the coast, that a palpable chill prevailed. The temperature called for warm clothes. But the sky was clear and bright with the slightly orange hue of a sun that had chosen a much lower station in the sky. Deep, long shadows were cast between the buildings. No clouds to speak of. All of this made for excellent visibility, from the relief mission as well as *at* the relief mission.

There had been no more shots. Richter had made his call, and NATO planes were back, overflying them within half an hour. They hadn't let up all night.

Frank, Richter and the two duty officers had picked up Dayna's limp body on a stretcher the day before and moved it to a gurney in the clinic. Gwen's ankle was too sore for her to help.

They wrapped the body in operating room drapes. Frank and Richter had surveyed the entry and exit wounds. The first was right in the middle of her sternum. The large exit wound was about six inches across. They came to the conclusion that the sniper had used an expanding bullet, one banned by international convention, but apparently in common use in Sarajevo.

The cruelty of humans never ceased to amaze Frank.

Soon, dealing with Dayna's body was going to become more than unpleasant.

The evening had gone quickly. Taking care of Gwen's ankle. Getting something to eat. More taking care of her ankle. Then to bed.

Frank remembered his nightmare. He knew he'd had them before but didn't always remember them. This one he did, and it sent a shiver up his spine. He was slowly starting to remember others.

He was tending to Gwen's ankle after getting them breakfast. He heard the whistling roar of a jet approaching and quickly ran to the window.

Separating the shutters, he saw the Canadian F-18 pass overhead and just clear the next hilltop. Looking from behind, he could make out the grey exhaust in the bright sunlight.

He went back to Gwen and took off the warm compress. Once again, there was a lot of puss.

He said, "This has to hurt. A lot."

"It's not that bad. I can handle it. For now."

He could see the way she tried to hide her wince when she talked about it or he handled her ankle. A small change, but he saw it. He said, "You're full of shit. I can see your reaction from across the room. I'm going to get you something for the pain."

"No," Gwen said loudly. "I'm not having that. I won't take any." She waved the idea away with the broad stroke of her hand. "I need all my wits about me. That kind of thing just won't do."

"God, you're a hard one." He thought a moment and turned toward her. "Maybe that's what I like about you."

She chuckled and smiled. For a moment she seemed a little impish. That too faded quickly.

Frank checked his watch and said, "I have to go see Richter and find out what NATO has planned for us."

"Be careful."

Frank strode confidently across the square, slowing only to look down at the massive spill of dried blood that was attracting so many flies. He never slowed completely, staring back on the red patch, unable to divert his eyes. Wishing they could have cleaned the gravel somehow. He was so upset about the flies that he wanted to go back and squash all of them. Make death agonizing for each and every one of *them*. He was fighting with himself not to go back because he couldn't stand there, being a target for someone to shoot. He could barely make himself get to the main door. Looking back at the flies swarming around the red patch on the ground, feasting on Dayna's spilled blood.

They're consuming her!

He almost turned back but felt his hand on the door. Frank opened the door slowly and looked inside. He took a last look at the red patch and thought he felt the flies swarming on his back. He swatted at his back and realized what he had just done. He let the door slam behind him and went up the stairs, chuckling just as he entered Richter's office.

Richter, standing behind his desk, suffused in the golden morning glow off the tarpaulin, turned to him and snapped, "What's so funny?"

Frank stopped himself and said, "I'm coming up the stairs and I said to myself, *Gonna see, Colonel Almost Lost His Head.*" He started to chuckle again. "You remember? The bullet? You stepping forward?" He laughed and shook his head slowly.

"Really?" Richter scowled.

Father John, in front of the glowing tarp, surrounded by a surreal glow, said, "Not funny." Loudly, as if he was admonishing someone, "Not funny at all!"

Frank turned to him and shrugged with his palms open.

"You're shell-shocked," Father pointed at him, "or something."

Frank started to laugh again. He couldn't help himself.

Richter, understanding the situation, put his arm around Frank's shoulder and walked him over to one of the green leather chairs. He helped him sit.

Frank laughed even harder, leaned back into the chair, howling, and just as suddenly crumpled forward with his face between his knees and started to sob uncontrollably.

Richter sat on the arm of the chair and pulled Frank's head onto his shoulder, comforting him.

Father John edging closer, watching.

"It's okay," said Richter, rubbing Frank's other shoulder. "Let it all out."

Frank was unable to stop with his face in the nape of Richter's neck. Trying, but unable to pull himself together. Then he felt a third hand rubbing his back and his head. The heat from the radiant glow of the tarpaulin didn't do him any good. Feeling Richter rubbing his shoulder. Unable to escape from the dark hole that was his cold soul.

It went on for some time.

Father John looked at Frank and then at Richter with disbelief.

Finally, Richter said softly, "I have news. Good news."

Slowly, Frank stopped sobbing. He turned up to Richter and said, "Really?"

"Yes."

Frank pulled away, settling into the back of the chair and rubbing his red eyes.

Richter went to his desk and sat on the near edge. Father John grabbed the other chair.

The left shoulder of Richter's khaki shirt was soaked with tears, with streaks down the front to which he didn't pay any attention. He said, "I have word from UNPROFOR that we are being evacuated tomorrow morning."

"What," said Frank in a shout of amazement. "How?"

"Thank God," said Father John.

Richter explained. "Helicopters are coming from Ramstein, by the back way across Italy and Switzerland."

"They'll get shot down," said Frank.

"Well. No. There's going to be an *exercise* over the Adriatic of combined fighter forces overflying Yugoslavia with anti-radar missiles. There will be planes from the *Theodore Roosevelt* and from Aviano."

"Really?" said Frank.

"General Carter spoke to me from Ramstein late last night." said Richter. "The operation is being run by General Carter, personally. It's his idea. I believe you know him."

"Yes." Frank sat back in his chair with a tremendous sense of relief.

"And get this. The helicopters are from Germany, France, Italy, England, the United States and Russia." Richter let it sink in. "The mission has top-level political clearance from all nations involved. Including Canada, who will be flying with the Russians. This way, when the shit hits the fan at UN Security Council, they will all be in it together. Hopefully they'll tell the UN to fuck right off." Richter gazed up at the ceiling. "Did I just say that?"

"Forgive him, Lord," said Father John.

"Damn, Vern Carter," said Frank.

"The first plane arrives at exactly 0847hours."

A jet fighter flew over the compound.

FORTY-SIX

Kamenko Hradich was sitting at a roadside café, alone. It was almost four o'clock. In front of him sat a cup of black coffee, delightfully sweetened, and a tumbler of slivovitz. Two other men sat three tables away.

He longingly took a last drag of his cigarette and dabbed it out in the glass ashtray. He let the smoke go slowly, and immediately reached into his pocket for another one. He lit it reflexively with a lighter from his other pocket.

He was so absorbed in his thoughts.

The last week had gone very well. They had cleared two more villages. In all, burying several hundred men and dispersing the women. Some of his men had their way with the women.

But that was their right. Their reward.

He had almost shot Colonel Richter. Silently he cursed his luck that the German had stepped forward. In the seconds it took his bullet to travel the distance, the damned colonel had stepped forward to address that other bastard, Frank Lambert. At least he had hit the one he thought was Father John. Hraditch just didn't know how bad the wound was.

Oh well, it was a quick second shot.

His sergeant had taken out the man who brought Frank Lambert back in the old jalopy of a truck. Used an anti-tank rocket. The Americans called them bazookas.

Worked well, though.

The man was probably a farmer from near the field where they had beaten Frank almost to death. He remembered when they heard the truck approaching and the surgeon was lying on the ground, unconscious. He had wanted to pull the trigger, but something held him back. He had been certain the cold, the injuries and animals would have finished him off. Now, Hradich regretted not killing him. In his position, you could never be too careful. Oh well. What could he do? As for the farmer, they'd go back and figure out who he was. Find his family.

He smiled,and thought, *We'll fix them right up.*

He looked at his glass. It was almost empty. He turned to see the waiter coming out the stone archway to the other table.

"Hey, boy," he shouted. "Can't you see my glass is empty."

"Yes, colonel. Sorry."

"Fill it." He scowled. "Doesn't anybody around here know how to work anymore?"

"Yes, yes." The waiter quickly left the other table.

A moment later he was back, free pouring slivovitz into Hradich's glass.

Hradich reached for the waiter's wrist and held it firmly. Staring malevolently at him.

The dark-haired boy warily pulled his hand away and left.

His cigarette nearly done, Hradich stabbed it hard into the ashtray. It made a loud clank on the metal table. Just as quickly, he lit another one.

And the big black cook. *That was a beautiful shot.*

The one that irked him the most was Frank. Although, the surgeon had spared him the agony of a grandchild that was half the enemy—an eternal damnation—a cross to bear. Hredich knew now—that's why he hadn't shot Frank.

He sucked on his cigarette and contemplated the glowing ash.

Still, the doctor had turned traitor on him. Taking girls from other people. Not clearing it with him. Hradich. He was the UN Liaison.

The whole thing with the UN stank. Coming to his country to tie their hands. Meddling in their affairs.

Who do they think they are?

Would they even think about meddling in the affairs of France or Germany? Or Canada or the United States? Of course not. They came to Yugoslavia to get their hands dirty—to feel satisfied—like they had done something.

Hah!

Now there were rumors that they would go to Afghanistan. Hadn't they learned from the Russians? Would Frank want to go there? Did he feel the need to go there?

He took a deep pull of his slivovitz.

There was still time to fix up Frank and everybody else on the hill. Especially Frank. An idea came to him. He would get the men together.

Hradich drained his glass, threw down an American bank note and quickly left.

FORTY-SEVEN

Colonel Richter sat in his rocker, alone. He had no lamps on. The order was *lights off*, to avoid any trouble with snipers. Still, his eyes had acclimatized to the dark and the tarpaulins let in just enough light.

They were going to be rescued in the morning. Evacuated by helicopters from six nations. Without UN sanction.

Gebrochener eier. (Egg on their face)

He chuckled.

The most important thing was to get everybody out safely. He knew that depended largely on the helicopters and their armament. He didn't completely understand what was happening over the Adriatic in the morning. But if General Carter lived up to his reputation…

He fished into his bottom desk drawer and pulled out the bottle with the softly rounded edges, and a glass. He had brought four bottles with him. He had learned how to *pack* a large duffel. Three brandy and one Delamain. The Brandy was for others… He shook the cognac bottle. About two inches left.

I can handle that.

He poured some into a glass and savoured the explosion in his mouth.

Richter was saddened by Dayna's death. But what was done was done. The problem was what Jennifer had told him—*die schwarze*, was becoming a problem. Disapproving, not liking her, suspicious.

It was still too bad she had been killed.

He took another pull and refilled the glass.

At least, now, Jennifer was free.

He had made certain that she had been on this mission, just as on the previous three. They had a good thing going. They understood each other. And she had never failed him. He knew she had failed the American commandos, but she had never failed him.

The last take was a little meagre. Only four hundred dollars. Half the proceeds—or was it? But he had to trust her. The trouble was, the gig hadn't lasted long enough.

That was his final take on her.

He poured the rest of the cognac into his glass.

As for the drug money, the five thousand dollars for the antibiotics,... he'd had Mike, the duty sergeant, sign the cash ledger.

Richter never entered an amount, because Mike was just so sloppy. Always rushing for another cigarette. He didn't even notice.

Father John was no problem because Richter knew he had a past he wanted to hide.

As for Frank Lambert, he clearly had post traumatic stress disorder. So did Gwen Pakin. He was sure the ledger would stand. No matter what he wrote in it for the drugs they never got. Like seven thousand five hundred dollars.

FORTY-EIGHT

The USS *Theodore Roosevelt* was sailing west into the wind, about fifty nautical miles off the Bosnian coast.

On the deck were three F-18 As, armed and hooked up to the catapults. Wisps of steam, golden in the morning sun, escaped from the launchers near the front landing gear of the aircraft. Blast deflectors were up behind them. More F-18s stood behind, engines running. The tail fins were painted blue with a stencil image like the Wall Street bull, turning to charge. The letters A/C stood out.

The closest fighter to the aircraft carrier's island had stencilling under the closed canopy that read *Blackjack*. The pilot was looking up to his right at the port windows of the bridge. So was the shooter on the deck.

The pilot was watching the admiral, who had a phone to his ear. Waiting for his signal.

The admiral finally put his phone down and signalled the pilot and the shooter. With a big smile, he put two clearly visible thumbs up.

The pilot, smiling under his visor, returned two thumbs up. He took the joystick in his right hand as he turned his attention to the shooter.

The officer in the yellow vest, looked at the pilot and waved his hands around above his helmeted head.

The pilot moved the joystick through a full three hundred and sixty degrees.

With all control surfaces on the aircraft moving, the shooter bent his arms to ninety degrees at the hips and pivoted stern to bow.

The pilot relaxed his head back on the rest and pushed the throttles full forward. The plane shook like a coiled reptile as the engines spooled up. With his right hand he pressed the pickle, the control button on top of the joystick.

In two seconds the plane was hurtled off the end of the deck, leaving at nearly two hundred knots. Afterburners for a few seconds, and he was rapidly gaining altitude. Within a few minutes he levelled off at twenty thousand. Momentarily, two other F-18s came up beside him, one on either side. The flight commander searched the sky around him for bandits.

Satisfied, the pilot signalled, "Rough Rider, Rough Rider, this is Blackjack."

"Blackjack. Rough Rider copies."

"Moon and Rocky with me. Heading seventy-five degrees, three hundred eighty-five knots. Airspace clear. AWACS confirmed, one hundred miles south. Sat-Com linked. Negative civilian air traffic." There was a little bit of chirping from his radar warning. "Trivial hits from SAM radar."

"Blackjack, Rough Rider copies and advises Fighter Squadron 494 joining you, ETA nine minutes. Approaching from two hundred eleven degrees at sea level plus fifty."

Three more planes joined the flight commander in formation.

"Rough Rider, Blackjack advises Tank, Thunder and Scrapper are in formation."

He looked over at Thunder and saw that Janet was looking at him, the sun reflecting off her visor. When she held her thumb up, he returned the gesture.

"Blackjack," a different voice. The admiral. "Rough Rider says good hunting. Do your papa proud."

He answered the man he respected and obeyed more than anyone else, "Rough Rider, Blackjack says ten-four."

The flight commander surveyed the shimmering morning light of the Adriatic. He saw the other five F-18s around him and marvelled at their menacing beauty. He turned his attention north at the distant shore of Yugoslavia, a grey-green line stretching across the northern horizon.

The six jets banked right through a full half turn.

They flew on for a few more minutes. The sky was clear coming up on the carrier below.

Then he saw it. About twenty-five miles south. A long white line approaching across the Adriatic. That would be the 494, leaving shock waves on the ocean, flying fifty feet above the water. *Pity any boats.*

"Blackjack, this is Rosinante, FS 494," came over the flight commander's headset.

He answered, "Rosinante, Blackjack copies." Then his curiosity got the better of him. "What kind of handle is that?"

He heard a chuckle and then, "Rosinante was Don Quixote's horse. 494 going to forty thousand for rendezvous."

He thought, *Fucker.*

The incoming planes suddenly turned skyward and spread out.

He gave the order and his six planes went skyward to join the others. They formed a line stretching almost ten miles. Thirty aircraft. Every third one from the carrier.

The flight commander looked at the F-15s they had joined, the letters "LN" and a red stripe across the outboard tail fins. He noticed their ordnance and thought, *One huge wall of death flying north. If anybody wants to engage. Well...*

The radar warning chirps came more often and then became continuous.

FORTY-NINE

Morning came, and the anticipation was palpable. So was the anxiety. Nobody stepped outside. Duffel bags were packed and ready. People were watching out of cracks in their doors. All the medical equipment was being left behind. General's orders.

A beautiful clear morning with no hint of clouds, and yet…

Bright sun full of promise.

Frank took it to heart. All of this was going to be over soon. He was going back to the States with Gwen to start a new life—and nothing was going to stop him.

He had her on a draggable stretcher that he had fashioned himself from the top of a gurney. Since last night the pain had been so intense, she couldn't walk any more. And she still wouldn't take anything for the discomfort. But Gwen had her reason—wanting to be clear and alert. She was just inside the door, lying on the floor. He'd drag her out to the helicopter and hoist her on.

The plan was that Frank and Richter would evacuate last, once all the others had been taken care of.

He peered out the door. Silence. Just a glorious fall morning. No movement anywhere in the hills that he could see. The air was cool.

There had been no more jets since the one yesterday.

Not needed.

He sat down on the floor beside Gwen and stroked her hair, like he had done so many times before.

They didn't say anything. Just the odd sigh from Gwen.

Frank checked his watch. 0830. Seventeen more minutes. The choppers would be four minutes apart.

***

The pilot kept the F 18 low over buildings and trees as he hid from the SAM's radar. Two planes had been fired upon. One was damaged but managed to get back to the carrier. Now he was being targeted by a site near the mission their forces were going to evacuate. The Bosnian Serbs would kill the rescue helicopters.

He kept the jet just above stall speed as he waited for his answer from the carrier.

His headset crackled, "Blackjack, strike authorised."

"Ten four, I'm going in."

He turned on the air to ground missile and set it in SP mode. His radar system would fire it.

He banked left toward the spot he knew the SAM site was. Thirty seconds and with a bit of throttle he brought the jet up.

His warning system chirped radar hits.

The missile dropped from the plane and suddenly streaked forward.

He throttled back to take the jet lower. Before he could there was a bright flash ahead of him and the radar warnings stopped.

The Flight Commander was going to take out the control truck too. He switched on his gatling gun. The target grid came up in the heads up display. He saw his quarry beyond a peaked building on a hilltop and targeted it for one hundred rounds. He pushed the pickle. In the second that it took to release the volley, the slow moving jet caught a down draft.

The roof of the building on the hill top was being shredded at the same time as his target.

Shit!

***

Frank heard what he thought was a sonic boom outside. He cracked the door open. There was a flash to the east.

Gwen sat up. "What is it?"

He saw the roof of the main building across the square cut to ribbons with small explosions. Debris scattered. One piece hitting their door. There was smoke.

An F 18 passed just over top of the building, going east.

"Friendly fire," he shouted at Gwen. "We're getting collateral damage."

Richter's in the building!

He turned back to her. "Got to go."

"What..."

Frank ran across the square just as Richter stumbled out the door, coughing, followed by billowing smoke.

He got to the colonel and saw the bleeding from the right side of his chest. Frank dragged him back to the edge of the stone building and sat him down on the gravel. Richter seemed dazed. He peeled back his shirt and assessed the wound. Deep but not serious.

"Kurt, look at me." Richter seemed to focus. "I'm going inside to get a bandage for this." He waited a moment. "Stay here."

Frank entered the building and opened the door to the clinic. The ceiling was partly gone and he could see blue sky above. The smoke was clearing. Nothing was shifting.

What the hell.

He went in and grabbed some gauze dressings, some micropore roles and some rubbing alcohol.

Back outside, Richter seemed recovered. He said, "Thank you," and placed his hand on Frank's.

"Never mind." He doused the wound in alcohol, which made Richter wince, and covered it in gauze. He pulled the blood-stained shirt over the bandage.

He looked at Richter. "The building's stable. Get inside. I'm going back."

***

On the far side of the hill to the east of the relief mission, Hradich lay waiting. He hoped the pilot hadn't seen him or the few men with him when he flew over. Otherwise, he could come back north to south and eradicate them in seconds.

He knew the surface to air missiles were gone. That was too bad. He also knew that all this activity must mean a rescue attempt was coming—soon.

I won't let it happen.

If rescue helicopters came, they would fly up the valley for cover, and quickly get up to the village. Hradich and his men wouldn't be seen.

He was waiting for the rest of his men to arrive with their mortars.

Maybe we can get them all. Especially Doctor Frank.

***

Frank was back inside with Gwen and explained the situation to her. He thought the evacuation fleet would know what had happened and would arrive late. It was already 0851.

On a whim, he decided to give her his journal. He pulled it out of his duffel and went to her.

"This is a journal I've been keeping of all the cases we've done here. I didn't tell you about it."

"Why?"

"It's just something that I did, but now I think it's really important." He held up his hand to her. "You're going out first, so I'm putting it in your duffel—"

"Frank..."

"Let me finish. If something happens to me, and it won't, I want you to take it to the UN, or the media, or a publisher and make sure people know what's going on over here. What's happening to these girls."

He stuffed it into her duffel, hugged her and sat down on the floor.

Time crept like cold molasses spilling in an ice storm. He kept checking.

Gwen looked at him, as if she knew what he was thinking.

Frank suddenly remembered himself between the buildings, carving tents. For him that was the turning point. Improvising to treat the girls. In retrospect, though, his plan had become Hradich's. The guy obviously thought he owned it. But Frank? He wasn't being bought with slivovitz and empty words. If only he'd heeded his early misgivings about Hradich. He reminded himself that under these circumstances, you could never be sure of anybody or anything.

In the half sleep of the night before, he had even remembered his dreams and his flashbacks. All of them. He had been in Rwanda. He had been with his wife. And he had been with his father when he died. Never really understanding his hurt soul before. Everything coming together now. He'd be able to get it out and move on.

He thought he heard something. The sound of a helicopter? He strained to hear. Definitely a jet engine and rotors. His watch said 0905 hours. Looking out the door, it took a few moments. The aircraft suddenly appeared out of the valley, coming up over the rooftops of the deserted village that had been the mission, surrounding them in jet whine and rotor chops. A large Italian helicopter settling just outside the southeast corner of the square in a cloud of dust.

Richter was already outside, shouting orders and covering his face from the flying debris. His shirt torn on the right. He looked at Frank and pointed to the ground, obviously wanting Gwen.

Frank turned back and said to her, "Here we go, baby," and threw the door open wide. He dragged her out.

Seven support staff were rushing to the chopper with the open door.

Richter directed the first six to get on board with their duffels.

The far side of the helicopter was open too, occupied by an airman manning a heavy machine gun. He didn't take his eyes off the far hills.

The first six were on.

Richter shouted over the noise, "Let's get her in."

Richter winced as they lifted Gwen into the side of the aircraft on her stretcher. There was no more room.

Richter shouted to the last woman, "Next one, "directing her back to her building. He walked stooped over to the front and signalled the pilot with a wave of his hands.

The helicopter powered up and rose into the air. Frank could see that the passengers were being given headsets so that they could hear. The doors remained open. The pitch from the rotors changed and the aircraft banked and descended into the valley, disappearing from view over the run-down slate rooftops.

Frank rubbed the grit out of his eyes and could see Richter doing the same. Then he thought he heard something. Could it be a heavy machine gun, barely audible over the fading rotor chops? They had no communication with the rescue fleet.

Were the first group okay? Was Gwen okay? He had no way of knowing. He had a moment of panic.

Moments later, the square was barely quiet when Frank could hear another chopper approaching in the distance. Surely they wouldn't be coming in if there were problems. They'd call for jets. So it *was* probably just his imagination.

A German helicopter rose above the main building and quickly settled just off the square.

Frank turned and pushed his face against the side of his quarters to shield his eyes.

Richter was shouting for more people.

They ran out and clambered aboard with their duffels.

Richter gave the pilot the sign, and the chopper ascended and disappeared into the valley.

Frank knew that the pilot would have signalled Richter if there were problems.

There came a silence that Frank knew wouldn't last. He looked at Richter and felt a great admiration for him for getting his people out. When Richter finally acknowledged him from across the square, Frank stood and saluted him. For a moment Frank was proud of his military past.

Richter came to full attention and saluted back.

Then the cacophony of sound returned. Jet whine and rotor chops seemed to come from everywhere. A Russian chopper came up over the rooftops and settled just outside the square.

Richter was in the middle of it, already shouting orders.

More people were running out. Father John was with them, helping drag Dayna's broken body out, bending like it was hinged where her spine was shot through. The group threw her floppy body bag up through the door. Father John was a symbol of composure. Then he was into the plane and up and away, after Richter's order.

Frank was glad to see Father John go. He didn't know why but recognized his ambivalence toward the priest. And there was that girl who had looked at John with what seemed like suppressed horror. John had quickly turned away and nothing had come of it. But it did make

Frank wonder. It hadn't sat well with Gwen either when he had told her about it. Mistaken identity? They'd work *that* out back home.

Dayna was another matter. *Of all people, Dayna?*

Frank forgave himself for his thoughts about John and stood tightly tucked into the side of his quarters.

Richter stayed by the main building.

Just moments later the next helicopter rose out of the valley and shot debris in all directions as it settled in the square.

Frank turned out from the corner where he had buried his face. It was a French assault helicopter with a gatling gun mounted under its nose and missiles alongside. He watched Richter making his decisions and giving his orders. Only two people could get on board. That meant there were five people left.

Richter was a bit slow deciding, and he glanced over at Frank. Obviously something was on his mind. He finally gave the order for two others to board and the French copter went into the air and out of sight in the valley with the expected cacophony of sound.

With the chopper going low into the distance, the sound disappeared, and an eerie silence came over the village.

Frank checked his watch again and saw that the previous aircraft had actually been three minutes apart.

The silence lasted, and he strained for the next sign.

He saw Richter looking at him from across the square with a grave expression.

What would make him look like that? Was he thinking about Hradich? Dayna? The drug theft? Did he just want to have this over and done with? Or was he thinking about Frank?

***

Father John was sitting on the seat of the Russian chopper, just above Dayna's body bag. A Canadian airman had strapped the body down, so that it wouldn't tumble out the open door. A Russian gunner sat at the other open door.

John thought about Gail, in Baltimore. So many years ago. He had never taken confession for that. Never atoned. Then there was what had happened in Yugoslavia. He rested his head back on the aircraft's finely vibrating bulkhead. And the boys…

What bothered him the most, was knowing that Frank, evil Frank, had aborted *his* child. His only… Even if the mother hadn't wanted it. *Absurd!* A Catholic priest had a child that was aborted! And there was nothing he could have done about it.

His heart pounded like it was going to tear him apart. He took a deep breath. He felt confined and needed to stand.

Father John undid his lap belt, took the grab iron in his hand and stood up to look out the door at the amazing view. Fertile fields below and the craggy Alps in the distance. They were about five hundred feet above ground.

"Sir, sit down, *sir,*" Came over his head set. "Sir!" Insistence.

Father John turned around slowly, accommodating, to look at the Canadian airman. He motioned twice to the floor with his free hand and smiled.

He remembered Matthew's scripture, from the Berean Bible. Why the Berean Bible?

Many said, Lord look at all the good things I did. But the Lord said, depart from me, I never knew you.

John sighed. Finally, he had the answer to all his prayers.

He took a deep breath.

Father John let go the grab iron and vanished.

***

Time seemed to creep for Frank.

At last, the sound of a chopper coming.

The British craft came up and settled in the square just as quickly. Richter signalled Frank to come, as well as the last three personnel from the barracks.

They ran to the side of the aircraft.

An airman in the door was shouting something at Richter, who shook his head, shrugged his shoulders, and turned his hands to his ears.

Richter signalled the last three in and turned to Frank.

Under the engine whine and rotor noise, he shouted hard in his ear, "Get in!"

There was only room for four.

The rotor chops were like hammer hits on plywood coming from different directions.

Frank got up beside Richter's head and shouted, "No!"

Richter was in his face, forming his chevrons, deep with displeasure. He glanced at his right chest—his shirt flapping over the bandage the surgeon had placed.

Frank in his ear again. "You go with your people." He waved to the open door. "They're yours. Under your protection."

Richter slowly looked to Frank and screwed his mouth up, "Get in now. That's an order!" standing firmly as he was pelted with debris, pointing at the door.

The jet whine was deafening. The smell of burnt kerosene.

"Kurt," Frank shouted, "with all due respect, no. You go with your people. I'm the outlier. The Americans will be here in a few minutes. I'll fly with my air force. I belong with them." He pushed the reluctant colonel toward the door. "See you in Ramstein."

Richter looking like he knew things had to get moving, reluctantly took the grab bar and hiked his leg up. Frank pushed him up by the buttock and threw Richter's duffel into the helicopter.

Frank ran back to his corner and watched the helicopter rise into the air.

Richter was standing in the doorway, staring down unhappily at Frank as the craft rose skyward. It was as if they were still face-to-face. Frank was getting scolded. Connected by military protocol and Richter not letting go. Then the rotor sound changed and the chopper pitched sideways and disappeared like it was swallowed into a hole in the valley.

With it went all the noise, the smell of burned jet fuel and the dust.

Frank was left with a bit of a buzz. A ringing in his ears.

There followed an empty silence.

A space in which he was able to access his own soul.

Time seemed to move slowly again, now that he was on his own.

He thought about the horrors of Rwanda. The disembowelled bodies and the smell of rotting human flesh.

He wondered why he had anticipated one abortion after the other. How he had adjusted to it so easily.

He checked his watch.

He thought about the day his father died. How he had stood at the bottom of the hospital bed and watched the whole thing. How he had utterly and completely *forgotten* about it. He shook his head. More like his soul had buried it deep inside. Like a bad, brown corner of his lawn sitting on tainted soil, leaving just enough visible to vex him for the rest of his life.

He thought about life with his ex. He had completely buried that dream, which wasn't a dream at all.

Reality was beginning to overtake him. Now that he had remembered all this, it was like he had been liberated. Some great weight had been taken off his shoulders.

Everything would be better now. Especially together with Gwen.

Frank checked his watch again. In total, five minutes had gone by.

Why is it taking so long?

He breathed in deeply and felt a prickly tingle up his back.

Another agonizing minute of silence.

Momentarily, Frank thought he heard a chopper. Still some distance away. He strained to hear. Yes definitely a chopper. That would be the American craft. The sweet sound of jet engines and rotors—Coming for him.

Finally. A feeling of relief coursed through him, like a warm soothing, mulled wine on a cold winter's day. From his core, out to his finger tips.

He relished the feeling.

Then he thought he heard something else. Something far more sinister. Frank stepped out from the side of the building into the middle of the square and looked around. The morning sun was bright. The sky was clear. There was a continuous popping noise coming from the surrounding hills.

He checked around, straining to see or hear.

The main building just in front of him exploded.

Frank spun around to…

✳✳✳

Gwen lay on the floor of her helicopter next to the open door, looking out, watching the green rolling countryside come and go, seeing the distant snow-capped mountains getting closer. That would be Switzerland.

She had listened in on the whole operation on her headset, remarking at how well it had gone. All the chatter between the pilots and

252

the commander. Just a few bursts of gunfire at what were probably ghosts by anxious airmen.

Gwen had heard about Father John—that didn't trouble her. She knew Richter was on a plane, and Frank was getting picked up. But she'd feel better when she was sure.

She looked up. The head of the helicopter was shaking visibly.

The whole thing went through her mind again, in an instant. Chechnya. Rwanda. Bosnia.

Her headset crackled, "Leader One this is Rescue Six. Approaching co-ordinates."

More crackling. "Leader One. Leader One. Rescue Six circling co-ordinates. Verifying co-ordinates. Leader One, the village is gone."

"What?" She recognized General Carter's voice. "Rescue Six, say again."

Gwen couldn't believe what she was hearing. Her chest was heaving. She felt dizzy. Fists clenched tight, her nails dug into her palms, drawing blood.

"Leader One, Rescue Six advises the mission has been destroyed. Smoke. Fire. Debris. Multiple, multiple, explosive craters. Likely mortars. No sign of life. No body. Uploading images to you."

Gwen turned to her left to look out the door. Her mouth was open. Her heart raced.

A gritty tear crept over the bridge of her nose.

-End-

Author's Notes

I would like to thank my editor Shane Joseph, for his patience and guidance during the writing of this work. His suggestions have amplified the story at many levels.

There is the contribution to my understanding of Allied Forces Central Europe, made by my close friend Nelson Wagner.

Thanks also to Harvey Auman and his terrific recounting of his adventure with the necessary sack of sugar, during the Korean War.

I am indebted to the many military personnel who have spoken to me about their deployments around the world. For the relief workers who have spoken to me about their missions from Rwanda and Burundi to Chechnya and Afghanistan; their stories paint a compelling portrait.

I thank the men of the VA/72 for their friendship, their stories and for inviting me aboard their wonderful ship, the *USS John F Kennedy*, off of Montego Bay in 1975 and showing me its workings.

Last but not least, my wife and family for putting up with me during the writing.

Although this is a work of fiction, I have long felt compelled to tell the story of the sexual suffering of women during war. The problem ran rampant during the Bosnian conflict. Rape is a traditional weapon of war. An unfortunate one we need to eliminate.

Author Bio

Klaus Jakelski has been a practising physician since 1979. He graduated from the University of Western Ontario and from University of Toronto Medical School. Klaus has worked everywhere, from the emergency room to the operating room, from the hospital floor to the office floor. He continues to practice medicine and works assisting Sudbury's cardiac surgeons. In the past he has written columns for a local paper and recently retired from the board of Norcat, a technology incubator. He lives with his wife, Cathy in Sudbury, Ontario. Klaus is equally at home in the wilds of Georgian Bay and the North Channel or in big cities such as Toronto, Boston, and Berlin. ***Dead Wrong*** was his first novel.

www.ingramcontent.com/pod-product-compliance
Lightning Source LLC
Chambersburg PA
CBHW070623170726
48291CB00003B/849